'So, we meet avixen.'

Rees's hand closed fingers was subtle, a light but determined statement of possession, and she felt the colour drain from her face.

'What's wrong? Didn't you expect to see me?' his voice rasped in her ear, a darting mockery lacing the words.

She did not answer. If she had tried, no sound would have come from her achingly parched throat.

Dear Reader

The background in which a novel is set can be very important to a reader's enjoyment of the story. What type of background do you most enjoy? Do you like a story set in a large international city or do you prefer your story to be set in a quiet rural village away from the hustle and bustle of everyday life? What about exotic locations with hot climates and steamy lifestyles? Let us know and we'll do all we can to get you the story you want!

The Editor

When **Joanna Neil** discovered Mills & Boon, her lifelong addiction to reading crystallised into an exciting new career—writing romances.

Always prey to a self-indulgent imagination, she loved to give free rein to her characters, who were probably the outcome of her varied lifestyle. She has been a clerk, telephonist, typist, nurse and infant teacher.

She enjoys dressmaking and cooking at her Leicestershire home.

Her family includes a husband, son and daughter, an exuberant yellow Labrador, and two slightly crazed cockatiels.

Recent titles by the same author:

TREACHEROUS PATH

TOUCH OF FIRE

BY

JOANNA NEIL

MILLS & BOON LIMITED
ETON HOUSE   18-24 PARADISE ROAD
RICHMOND   SURREY   TW9 1SR

All the characters in this book have no existence outside the imagination of the Author, and have no relation whatsoever to anyone bearing the same name or names. They are not even distantly inspired by any individual known or unknown to the Author, and all the incidents are pure invention.

All Rights Reserved. The text of this publication or any part thereof may not be reproduced or transmitted in any form or by any means, electronic or mechanical, including photocopying, recording, storage in an information retrieval system, or otherwise, without the written permission of the publisher.

This book is sold subject to the condition that it shall not, by way of trade or otherwise, be lent, resold, hired out or otherwise circulated without the prior consent of the publisher in any form of binding or cover other than that in which it is published and without a similar condition including this condition being imposed on the subsequent purchaser.

*First published in Great Britain 1992
by Mills & Boon Limited*

© Joanna Neil 1992

*Australian copyright 1992
Philippine copyright 1992
This edition 1992*

ISBN 0 263 77730 8

*Set in Times Roman 11½ on 12 pt.
01-9209-44640 C*

Made and printed in Great Britain

CHAPTER ONE

WHAT on earth had possessed Sam to put the supplies way out of reach on the top shelf? Katherine asked herself moodily, letting her glance skip over the endless assortment of brown cardboard boxes. Tentatively, she adjusted her precarious foothold on the ancient step-ladder. The clutter at high level wasn't much different from the state of the rest of his office—the least he could have done was to stay around just a few minutes to help her find what she was looking for.

Not Sam. 'Got to rush,' he'd said. 'Appointment at three. Have a rummage around, the samples are in there somewhere. Can't say I've heard many success stories with the new ointment, but that's people for you—odd customers, most of 'em. The old man'll probably find it does wonders for horses. Don't forget to check the locks before you leave—and when you get back to Fairoak tell Digby it's time he looked me up.'

'Will do,' she'd offered to his retreating back.

She sighed now, surveying the crowded shelves. Sam might well be a leading light as chief pharmacist for a major drug company, but he was the untidiest man she had ever come across. It didn't bother him, of course. His office was in a little block set apart from the rest of the buildings on site, and he was quite content to spend his days in isolated and splendid disorder.

Why couldn't he have hung about for a while? It might have been reassuring to know that he was there to see that she didn't break her neck on his rickety ladder. Judging by the state of it, she'd be lucky if she escaped with multiple fractures—she wouldn't care to bet that its birthplace wasn't the original ark. Carefully, she inched one foot on to the topmost step.

'Need any help?' The distinctly gravelled male tones cut across the silence, making her jump. Beneath her the whole fragile structure rocked ominously and she made a grab for the supports at either side.

Holding on to the frame with grim effort as it steadied, she cautiously twisted around, and found herself staring down into a pair of vividly gleaming blue-grey eyes. The breath momentarily snagged in her throat. It was the shock, she told herself, of finding that she had unexpected company.

Slowly she exhaled, blowing the wayward tendrils of honey-blonde hair back from her forehead so that she could get a better look at the intruder.

The eyes, she discovered, belonged to a ruggedly chiselled face, a strong nose and hard jaw framed by crisp black waves. Underlying the tanned surface of his skin there was a definite dark area. Designer stubble, she decided. He probably needed to shave twice a day.

He looked, at the same time, faintly disreputable and dangerously male, and his unheralded presence in the small office was beginning to have a thoroughly unsettling effect on her. Studying him, Katherine frowned. Somehow his face seemed vaguely familiar, yet, try as she might, she couldn't quite place him.

'Those heels aren't exactly the thing for climbing, are they?' he remarked, his gaze wandering with undisguised interest along the silk-smooth length of her nylon-clad legs to the three-inch stilettoes that encased her feet. 'You're not the pharmacist, are you?'

'I'm not. How did you get in?' she enquired shortly, cutting off his lingering scrutiny with a frosted glare.

He shrugged, broad shoulders moving beneath a grey leather jacket. 'The...door?' he murmured questioningly. 'It seemed like a good idea at the time. Are you the assistant, perhaps?'

She shook her head. 'I thought it was locked,' she muttered. 'Damn.'

A half-smile tugged at his mouth. 'I could do that for you,' he said, his tone bland. 'It's really no trouble.'

'No,' she said, her body jerking in negation. 'I mean, I wasn't expecting anyone.' The stepladder tilted with her agitated movements, threatening to dislodge her, and he came forwards, large hands catching her waist in a firm grip. Her scrambling fingers encountered leather.

'Is there a problem?' he murmured. 'My being here seems to be bothering you a little. Have I stumbled on to a robbery, or some such?'

He moved back slowly, taking her with him, and she lost her balance altogether and lurched forward, sliding down his long body until her feet touched the floor. His hands steadied her.

'R-robbery?' she repeated, her mind strangely confused, a small, ragged line furrowing her brow.

'Ah,' he said, his voice a pleasant undertone. 'Don't worry. I won't tell a soul.'

'What——?' The line etched itself deeper. Why wouldn't her brain function? Her senses were fogged all of a sudden, as though she were trying to find her way through a mist.

'You can trust me,' he said. 'I'll help.' His glance flickered. 'For a price...'

The mist cleared and Katherine yelped, hopping back as though she had been scalded.

'Don't be ridiculous,' she hissed. 'And—and let go of me. What do you think you're doing?' He was laughing at her, the wretch.

He released her, the smile still pulling at his firm mouth. The subtle fragrance of his aftershave remained to tease her nostrils, mingling with his own intrinsic male scent, and a hint, very faint, of something else.

She said abruptly, 'You've been drinking.'

'Lord save us,' he breathed, 'the world will end.'

'Is there a reason you're here?' Katherine asked, ignoring his sarcasm. 'It's the weekend, this place is closed. Perhaps you hadn't realised.'

'I knew that,' he said. He moved away from her and began to wander around the room, letting his glance flit in desultory fashion over the storage units that adorned the walls.

Watching him, Katherine chewed at her lip. Somehow she had to get rid of this man. Sam would not want a stranger lurking about the premises in his absence.

'Maybe I could help you in some way?' she suggested.

'I doubt that,' he replied. 'Unless you can produce a bottle of aspirin from somewhere.'

She blinked. 'If that's all you want, wouldn't you have done better to go to a chemist?'

He picked up a glossy magazine from a table and flicked casually through its pages. 'Probably,' he murmured. 'Except that a friend asked me to call in on Sam as a favour if I was in the area. He said it would save him a journey.' Losing interest, he tossed the book down on to the polished surface of the desk. 'It was only the headache and the thought of aspirin that reminded me to call in here.'

'I see,' Katherine said. 'What a pity you didn't think to give him a call and arrange to meet him. You might have saved yourself some trouble.'

'I understood that he liked to spend Saturday afternoon sifting through his paperwork.' His attention was diverted by a large and well-thumbed volume of pharmacopoeia, and Katherine observed him with growing irritation as his finger strayed idly through the contents.

'He had to go somewhere,' she said bluntly. 'It appears you're right out of luck today.'

He straightened and fixed her with a speculative regard. 'Seems that way, doesn't it? Still, you never can tell what might be around the corner.' His mouth crooked, and she knew a moment of misgiving, a strange fluttering sensation against her ribcage.

Once again she had the feeling that she had seen this man somewhere before. The same tall, lean frame had drawn her glance on more than one occasion, she was sure of it. Those eyes, brilliant with keen intelligence, played a haunting game of hide-and-seek with her mind.

She vied with the problem for a few seconds, fragments of images snatching at her memory.

'Is something wrong?' His dark brows came together, his expression serious now, the angle of his head alert.

She stared at him. 'No, nothing,' she began, and then her throat closed on the words as her mind made the swift leap of recognition.

It couldn't be him, could it? Rees Alton? He was away, working, he wasn't due back for some time yet. What would he be doing here?

She'd never actually met him, even though she had moved to a cottage bordering the Alton Estate. He was very rarely at home, always on the move from one assignment to the next, and so far their paths had never crossed. From time to time, though, his face would appear on the TV screen as he gave reports from various parts of the world where trouble had erupted. That must be the reason he had seemed so familiar to her.

He moved to half sit, half lean on the desk, his long fingers curling around the edge, and the way he was looking at her, the flicker of curiosity stirring the depths of his eyes, made her acutely uncomfortable. She said quickly, 'There may be some aspirin in the drawer. Sam sometimes keeps odd bits and pieces in there. I'll have a look.'

Pulling on the handle, she glanced at the mess inside, conscious that he had tilted his head to look with her. 'No, nothing in there,' she murmured, and slammed the drawer shut. He gave a shout of pain.

'What's wrong?' she asked, her eyes widening, her mouth dropping open.

'My finger,' he said, nursing his hand in his other palm. 'You just rammed it.' He inspected the digit closely. 'I think there's a splinter in there.'

'Oh, I'm sorry,' she muttered, biting her lip. 'I didn't realise your fingers were in the way. Perhaps you shouldn't be sitting on the desk.'

He glowered at her and she regarded him with uncertainty. This man wasn't Rees, was he? He couldn't be—David would have told her if he was expected back. After all, as Rees Alton's estate manager, David would surely be the first to know if he was about to descend on them. They would have abandoned their plans for this evening if there had been just a hint. It was one thing to hold an event on the property in Rees's absence, it was quite another to thrust it upon him without warning.

She swallowed. 'You... remind me of someone,' she said cautiously. 'Someone I've seen on TV. Do I know you? Are you Rees Alton?'

'You don't know me,' he said, a scowl hardening his mouth.

'But you——'

'Does it make a difference?' he gritted, clamping his teeth together. 'Why is it everyone goes wild to meet someone who's appeared on TV? Does a man or woman become suddenly more glamorous, worth rubbing shoulders with?'

His sharp tone made Katherine hesitant. 'I'm sorry. It's just that, well, you do look like him, and you have to admit, his lifestyle is something out of the ordinary——'

'So I've been told—frequently.'

He turned brusquely, and laid his hands on the back of Sam's chair, his jaw moving in a grimace.

'I didn't mean to pry, or intrude in any way,' she murmured in apology.

'No one ever does. I might be having dinner with friends, or a quiet drink in a pub, but that doesn't seem to stop them. If I've been on the move for hours on end, and all I want to think about is getting my head down somewhere quiet, you can guarantee there's always someone who will barge right in and bombard me with questions.'

Katherine moistened her lips. 'I should think that most people are naturally curious. They don't mean any harm, I'm sure.' She slanted him a brooding glance. 'That's the price of fame.'

'You may be right,' he said grudgingly. 'Most of the time, I suppose, being accosted by strangers doesn't bother me over-much. Right now, though, I can do without it.' He scraped a hand over his temple and pushed the chair to one side so that he could sit on it. 'Where did we get to with the aspirin situation? Any chance of a decent cup of tea around here?'

'Try a café,' she advised him shortly. 'I have no idea where Sam keeps his kettle. It could be in the filing cabinet for all I know.'

He grunted, and swung his long legs up on to the table, crossing them at the ankles. Leaning his head back on the upholstered leather of the chair, he closed his eyes.

Katherine watched him narrowly. This man couldn't possibly be Rees Alton. Why had she ever entertained the thought that he was anything like the cool, level-headed journalist who delivered such concise, and sometimes harrowing reports through the medium of television? He was nothing like that man. In fact, he bore more resemblance to a grouchy bear who had returned from a trip to find his lunch had been purloined.

'You can't stay here,' she said. 'You'll have to find somewhere else to sleep off your hangover.' She sniffed. 'Though I would have thought it rather early in the day to be having that kind of problem.'

He considered her from beneath thick, dark lashes, smoke-grey eyes assessing her thoughtfully. 'Don't give me any flak, lady,' he warned. 'I've had a hell of a day, and I'm in no mood for sniping.'

'Then the sooner you leave, the better. That way, we can both rest easy.'

'Aspirin?' he repeated, one black brow lifting slightly, and she let out an exasperated breath.

'I dare say I have a couple somewhere.' She retrieved her bag from the desk and sifted through its contents until she found what she was looking for. 'Yes, here we are.' She started to offer the two small tablets, but then her fingers closed on them and she said doubtfully, 'Perhaps you oughtn't to have these right away if you've had alcohol.'

His jaw clenched perceptibly. 'I thought you said you weren't the pharmacist,' he growled.

Katherine handed over the tablets. 'It's your life,' she said coolly, her chin lifting. 'If you start to feel odd and disorientated, don't blame me.'

He removed his legs from the table and stood up. 'If I do start to feel that way, you'll be the first person I think of,' he muttered. 'If you're not going to give me tea, I suppose I'd better find somewhere to wash these down.' He walked to the door.

'Try Westgate,' she said. 'There's bound to be a place along there.'

He sketched a brief salute. 'I'll do that. Give my regards to Sam if you see him.'

Katherine stared abstractedly at the door as it closed behind him. Despite the day's growth of beard that threatened his jaw and the lived-in look of his clothes, the likeness between that man and the journalist was uncanny enough to be disturbing.

Considering his boorish state of mind, it was just as well that he wasn't Alton. She dared not even think of what *his* reaction would be to arrive home and discover a barn dance taking place on his land.

Perhaps she ought not to have listened to David when he had said everything would be all right— but he had gone out of his way to convince her that he had full authority in Rees's absence, and in the end she had let herself be persuaded. When all was said and done, she needed the funds that the dance would bring in.

She braced herself, gathering her thoughts together. She really hadn't time to hang around here any longer, musing. There was still a drive of more than two hours ahead of her, and when she did finally get back to Fairoak a hundred and one things needed to be done before she could get ready for the dance.

A short while later, armed with the packages that Sam had put to one side for her, Katherine set the alarm on the office door and went to find her car. If the roads were fairly clear, she would arrive home in good time, and she could feed the animals in the refuge before going on to Digby's veterinary practice to take the evening surgery.

The refuge was rapidly becoming something of a problem, she reflected soberly. In the beginning she had thought nothing of tending the occasional injured wild animal that had been brought to her, and keeping it close by the cottage to oversee its progress had been the natural thing to do. The problem was that now most of the local people, as well as some from surrounding areas, knew that she would not turn them away if they arrived on her doorstep with some poor bedraggled creature in obvious need of care and attention. What they didn't think about was just how costly and demanding these little invalids could be.

Guzzler was a case in point. The tiny orphaned fox cub needed constant monitoring, a bottle-feed four times a day—more, if he had his own way—and Katherine allowed herself to be hoodwinked by his plaintive sniffles. It would be some weeks, and he would be several pounds heavier, before he was ready to return to his earth.

If the barn dance went well, there might at least be enough money to cover the cost of cages and bedding, and possibly a few extras. The mounting food bill was something she'd have to cope with in the coming months, along with the rising price of medicines, though Digby had offered to help out with that.

Acknowledging the persistent dull ache in her forearms, Katherine shifted the bulky packages she was carrying in a vain attempt to distribute their weight more evenly. It was not an easy manoeuvre, and it was only as she caught sight of a man emerging from a nearby doorway, head lowered, intent on pulling something from his pocket, that she realised the operation was loaded with risk. Just how much risk became obvious in the next few seconds, and the rapid succession of the events that followed all merged into a confusing jumble in her mind.

'What the——?'

The aggrieved male voice impinged on her consciousness in a heart-sinkingly familiar way at the same moment that a soft, thudding collision succeeded in knocking the breath from her lungs.

'Look out——!'

Her strangled warning came too late. There was a metallic jangle as a bunch of keys propelled themselves from his hand, and, with a sense of fatality, she saw the uppermost of her parcels begin a slow and shaky detour towards the ground.

'Ouch!' The man jerked his foot from under the offending box and glared at her.

'It's you again——' Katherine's hold on the remaining packages faltered, and one by one they tumbled to the floor, ricocheting off his hard body. 'Oh——' she frowned at him in consternation '—I hope you haven't broken anything.'

'My foot, I think,' he said grittily.

She pressed her lips together. 'I meant the samples,' she muttered. 'Why didn't you look where you were going?'

He bared his teeth in a way that could have been interpreted as menacing. 'I could ask you the same thing,' he rasped.

She eyed him warily. If his foot was throbbing, he might be forgiven a display of temper. 'I'm sure you'll feel better in a moment or two,' she said. 'I'm sorry if my boxes attacked you, but you could have tried side-stepping me.'

'If I'd known you had your head in the clouds, I would have.' He threw her a vexed look. 'It seems to me that whenever I'm in your vicinity I end up with a pain somewhere or other. Is it something you have against me in particular, or do you bear an antipathy towards men in general?'

'Neither.' One delicately shaped brow rose. 'Do I take it that your headache hasn't cleared yet? You can hardly hold me responsible for that.' Her glance went pointedly to the sign over the doorway from which he had emerged. 'Dog and Gun'.

He smiled thinly. 'You were the one who recommended Westgate. If it eases your tender sensibilities at all, I suffered a non-alcoholic lager to wash the tablets down. What is it exactly that disturbs you about our local hostelries?'

'Nothing at all,' she murmured. 'Except that this particular one has just closed and I could have done with something bracing to alleviate the strain of bumping into you. It's perhaps just as well, though. I really ought to be getting home.'

'That goes for me, too.' He looked around. 'I had some car keys a minute ago.'

Katherine's gaze went to the litter of boxes on the pavement. 'There they are,' she said, catching a glint among the debris, and stooping to retrieve them. He moved at the same time, and as their heads clashed she saw a few stars and heard him faintly groan, and then she watched in disbelief as the keys slid unceremoniously through the slats of a drain.

He was clutching his head with his palm as she turned dizzily back to him, her green eyes widening with dismay.

'Don't tell me,' he breathed, his lips barely parted. 'Don't tell me. I don't want to know.' He raised his eyes heavenward. 'Lord help me, I haven't led such a wicked life, have I? What did I do to deserve this?'

Straightening, she cleared her throat. 'I don't think there's any chance of getting them back,' she said, rubbing at her temple. 'You do have another set, don't you?'

His voice was cool and rather clipped. 'Not on me.'

'On your car, then?'

'Hardly.'

She made a determined effort not to flinch under his withering scrutiny. 'Anyone with a modicum of forethought,' she intoned gravely, 'would have a spare key fixed magnetically to the underside of the car.'

'You're joking, I hope. If you imagine I'd take the chance of inviting a would-be thief to help himself to my car, you can think again.'

Katherine frowned. 'Well, then, as far as I can see the only other answer is to look through the phone book to see who can do a replacement set.'

'And knowing the way my luck has gone today,' he said with a wry grimace, 'it'll be half-day closing for every number I ring.'

'Are you always this pessimistic?' She surveyed him with curiosity, and thought she detected the ghost of a grin creeping across his mouth.

'Only when I've spent most of the night and part of the morning on a plane, endured countless delays, eaten cardboard food, and discovered after all that that the airline has managed to misplace my luggage. At other times I'm only mildly cynical.' He gave her a preoccupied stare. 'Of course, I hadn't met you then. Heaven alone knows what's in store for me now.'

The unhappy thought occurred to her that Rees Alton could have spent a day travelling back from goodness knew where. She studied his face closely. 'Are you sure you're not——?'

'Don't ask,' he said in a growl.

She smiled through her teeth, and checked her watch. She didn't have a lot of time if she was to make it back to evening surgery. 'What are you going to do about your keys?'

'We might as well follow your suggestion and go and find a phone box.' He started to pick up her parcels. 'These weigh a ton,' he complained. 'No wonder it feels as though my foot's been crushed.'

A pang of guilt ran through her. 'Can you walk?' she asked, taking a couple of the packages from him, then, 'We? You mean you want me to go with you?'

'Since this is all your fault, the least you could do is come along and keep me company while I get it sorted out.'

'I really don't have a lot of time,' Katherine began, but trailed off, seeing his expression. He turned and set off along the street, and as he hadn't relinquished the rest of her belongings she concluded resignedly that she had no choice but to follow him.

He found a phone box and she propped open the door while he made several fruitless calls. Eventually, holding the mouthpiece to his chest, he glanced at her and said, 'Apparently, I should be able to get a set from this place, but they have to contact the manager.' After a few more words to the person on the other end of the line he replaced the receiver and they stepped out on to the pavement.

'Your problems are solved, then,' Katherine said as they walked back towards her car.

'I wouldn't say that.' Moodily, he stared around him. 'I told you I was doomed today. The manager's gone off to a football match—they're not sure how long it will be before he gets back. At this rate I'll be stuck in town most of the night, and I still have some hours of driving to do before I get home.' His frown was accusing, and Katherine flinched.

Arriving at the place where her small red Metro was parked neatly alongside the kerb, she opened the boot and retrieved her parcels from him.

'Think on the bright side,' she said, injecting what she hoped was a degree of challenging optimism into her voice. 'If you've been on the move all day, it might be a good idea to stay over—book yourself into a hotel.' She finished stowing the parcels and turned to study him reflectively, her gaze drawn to his travel-worn clothes. 'You could take a shower—that might make you feel better—and then you could finish the evening off with a decent meal.'

He closed the boot with a bang. 'Why is it I get the impression I'm being insulted?' he queried drily, and she felt the slow flush of heat burn along her cheekbones.

'I—uh—can't imagine why you should think that,' she mumbled. 'All I meant was that if you've had a bad day so far you could perhaps turn it into something a little more satisfactory for yourself. Get an advantage out of adversity, so to speak.'

'Oh, really?' His gaze drifted over her, and there was a glint in his dark eyes that made her shift uncomfortably. He said, 'That idea hadn't occurred to me, I must admit. Though, I suppose, now you come to mention it, it could hold distinct possibilities.' He stared thoughtfully at his foot. 'There is, of course, one minor flaw in your suggestion.'

Katherine looked at him askance. 'Oh?'

'Mm,' he murmured. 'You see, I shall be quite alone, and that prospect doesn't appeal to me at all.'

Katherine tossed his objection to one side with a shake of her head, warm gold tendrils of hair rippling brightly. 'I'm sure you'll find someone to keep you company. I've no doubt you can be quite resourceful if need be—besides——' her mouth curved '—it's not too long till opening time.'

Moving around to the front of the Metro, she was startled to find his hand closing on her arm, effectively barring her passage. The shock waves from that warm, firm touch tingled through her nerve-endings and travelled on, along the length of her spine. Her insides gave an uneasy little quiver.

She looked down at his long fingers, and said carefully, 'If you'll excuse me, I have to go. I have things to do.'

He smiled, an attractive, dangerous smile. 'Leave them till another day,' he urged, his voice like honeyed silk.

'I can't do that, I'm afraid—I have responsibilities, things I must see to.'

'You could learn to delegate.'

Her lips quirked disdainfully. 'You might well find that an easy option—I'm afraid I don't share your ability to shrug all manner of obligations to one side. Anyway, why should I even want to?'

'To make it up to me for all the discomfort and inconvenience I've been put through today. You owe me,' he said.

'Do I? And do I take it that my spending the evening with you is meant to be some kind of repayment?' She used a scornful tone, but it was lost on him. There was only a devilish amusement reflected in the glitter of his eyes and the mobile curve of his firm mouth. She viewed him with growing apprehension.

'I'm sure,' he murmured, 'that we could pass the time in an agreeable way.'

'What exactly did you have in mind?'

'One or two things occurred to me—we could have dinner together; that might be a good start.' He paused, an imp of mischief flitting across his features. 'Or we could dispense with food for the time being—I could have that shower, and afterwards you could massage my foot...' He grinned hopefully. 'But I don't suppose you'd agree to that, would you?'

Her expression was glacial. 'You're right, I wouldn't.'

'I thought as much.' He pulled a wry face. 'Dinner, then?'

She looked down at the hand that still gripped her arm, and he let her go, waiting for her answer. Some people walked towards them, a noisy, high-spirited group, and her gaze lifted. A young woman glanced at her briefly, then transferred her appraisal to the man at Katherine's side. The glance turned to a stare, and Katherine said, raising her voice a notch, 'As I may have said before...Mr Alton...it just isn't your day, today, is it?'

The woman gaped and nudged one of her companions. 'It's him—the one on TV. Tracy, we've got to stop—look, it's Rees Alton.'

'Who——? Hey, you're right—hold on, everybody, I must get his autograph.'

The murmuring grew into a hubbub, and within seconds a small crowd had gathered around, avid interest quickening on their faces.

'When did you get back to England, Mr Alton——?'

'How long are you here for——?'

'Will you sign this for me, and this one for my cousin?'

'Rees——'

Katherine carefully extricated herself from the mêlée, and watched as, after a moment's hesitation, he began to write, his pen flowing over the paper in swift, firm strokes. He had obviously decided that it was expedient not to disappoint the girls, and she wondered on how many occasions in the past he had been called on to produce a false signature.

Her mouth twitched, and in that moment he caught her gaze over the rapidly swelling sea of people. His dark eyes filled with the promise of retribution, but as she opened her car door and slid behind the wheel she told herself that she was not afraid. Starting up the engine, she stopped only to blow him a kiss, before slamming the door shut and pulling out into the road.

In her rear-view mirror, as she moved away, she saw the dark fury and mingled frustration etched on his taut features, and laughed softly to herself.

She had escaped. Her instincts had told her to get away fast, to run from the man with the devil's smile, and now she was free. She did not trust him, not one inch, but worse than that there had been this niggling feeling that she might not be able to trust herself. He had altogether too much dangerous allure, a heady male vitality that could tantalise and make it all too easy to fall for his particular brand of charm.

The car gunned along the road as she put the miles, and him, behind her. She would never see him again, and for that she was heartily thankful.

CHAPTER TWO

'AREN'T you eating?' The light, well-modulated voice roused Katherine from her reverie, and she looked up with a start to find David's quizzical gaze resting on her. 'You looked as though you were miles away,' he added, his blue eyes full of humour. 'You must have been staring at that buffet table for a full five minutes without moving a muscle. Actually, I thought the selection was quite good.'

She glanced down at the empty plate in her hand and crinkled her nose. 'I suppose I'm not really hungry,' she murmured, with a faint smile. Strange, really, that she had no appetite, as she had not eaten since lunchtime.

The small band of musicians returned to the dais and began tuning up their instruments. Absently, Katherine picked out a lettuce leaf and began to nibble.

'Is that it?' David laughed. 'There's not enough there to feed a flea.' His fair hair shimmered in the light from the overhead lamps, and she wondered, not for the first time, why some young woman had not snapped him up long ago. He was a good-looking man, around the thirty mark, and he had a casual, laid-back manner that she envied. She wished some of her own tension would dissipate.

'Are you quite sure that Rees isn't going to arrive out of the blue?' she asked, her worried gaze travelling around the freshly painted barn as though the journalist might be conjured up out of the walls.

'It's OK. There's nothing to worry about.' David's foot began to tap to the beat of the music. 'He would have contacted me if he was on his way back. He always has before, if only to make sure that the housekeeper checks up on supplies.'

She acknowledged his words with a slight nod, and slid a small portion of quiche on to her plate. Between bites she said, 'It's just that...plans can change, and I'd hate——'

'Relax, enjoy yourself. The last I heard was a couple of days ago. He was in a real hot spot—practically on the front line—and I don't think there's any chance of the fighting dying down, so he's going to be there for some time.'

Despite the warmth of the July evening, Katherine shivered. How could a man live like that, in constant danger, never knowing what the future might hold? Here, in the quiet depths of the country, they were relatively sheltered from the grim reality of the tragedies being played out in far distant lands. It took men like Alton to bring it all home to them, and even then they remained a safe distance away.

'If you're only going to pick at that,' David's voice broke in on her sombre thoughts, 'why don't you put your plate down and come and dance with me? They're just about to start a new set.'

She gave herself a mental shake. There was no point in allowing this absurd sense of foreboding to take over and spoil what promised to be a lovely evening. The dry, clear night had encouraged a good turn-out for the dance, and everyone was in a happy party mood. She deposited her plate on the table and took the hand that David held out to her.

'I hope you realise,' she said, as they walked to the middle of the room, 'that I haven't a clue about country dancing. It's a good thing they're playing an assortment, or I'd be a complete disaster.' She winced as they found themselves at the head of a column of people.

'There's nothing to it,' David assured her with a grin. 'All you have to do is hop down the centre aisle with me, twirl around a few times, and then change partners.'

'You make it sound so easy,' she murmured. 'But, just to be on the safe side, you are wearing reinforced toe-caps, I take it?'

The music started up and there was no more time for talking, as he swept her along with him into the rhythm of the dance. Reaching the end of the row, they swirled into the formation, and it was only then that she became aware of a murmur, a flutter of attention in the group, and she wondered if she had missed a step somewhere, or if her buttons had come undone.

Carefully, she smoothed down the wayward flounces of her blouse, and checked the soft folds of her amber-hued skirt.

The momentary pause broke, and the dance went on, as though nothing had happened, except that now Katherine could sense a strange undercurrent surging through the assembled throng. Her glance went to the couple at the head of the column, and the breath froze on her lips.

It was not fair, she thought. It was not fair.

The man was smiling, waiting with his partner for the cue of the music. To anyone who did not know better it was a pleasant smile, an acknowledgement of the revellers' good humour and enjoyment, but Katherine was not taken in, not for one minute. Rees Alton was looking in her direction, and his gaze flickered, fusing hotly with hers, in a way that made her mouth go suddenly very dry.

Desperately she thought of escape, of taking to her heels and running from the barn, but even as the reckless urge swept over her she knew that it would be an act of pure folly. He would come after her, there was no doubt in her mind. She read it in his smouldering grey gaze and in the fractional movement of his lips as he started down the line towards her. Those eyes spelled out a warning that she would dismiss at her peril, and for the second time that evening she shivered, prickles of apprehension breaking out on her skin.

Frantically she dragged her attention from him, and scanned the dancers for David. Why didn't he deposit his partner with someone else and come and use some of his solid-gold charm over here? If ever there was a time when it could come in handy, this was it.

'So, we meet again, my green-eyed vixen.' Rees's hand closed on hers, and instinctively she tried to pull away. The pressure of his fingers was subtle, a light but determined statement of possession, and she felt the colour drain from her face.

'What's wrong? Didn't you expect to see me?' his voice rasped in her ear, a darting mockery lacing the words.

She did not answer. If she had tried, no sound would have come from her achingly parched throat. Once again, with panicked haste, her eyes sought out David.

Rees watched her, then shifted in keeping with the music, and swung her around, his strong, muscular thighs brushing against hers. Her limbs were already shaky, and her step faltered. His arm tightened around her waist.

'Don't try fainting on me, sweetheart,' he gritted, his voice low and even. 'You're not going to wriggle out of this one so easily. I want to know what's going on—what the hell you and your friend, David Jenner, have been cooking up between you.'

He handed her on to her next partner, and, like an automaton, she followed the pattern of the dance, wishing it would end, so that she could get away; hoping it never would, so that she didn't have to face him again.

Why, oh, why hadn't she listened to her own misgivings, and called the whole thing off at the last moment? But she couldn't have done that; it had been too late, hadn't it? A lot of the tickets had been sold in advance, and she could hardly have cancelled a couple of hours before the start. Could she?

It was his fault, anyway, she told herself peevishly. If he had told her who he was, instead of making her go through that—that charade—she might have been able to do something about it. It would have given her a few hours' grace, at any rate. She might have phoned David and sorted something out.

Her mouth firmed. If he was going to come back like this, without any warning, he deserved an unsettled welcome.

As the music came to an end, David met up with her once more. 'Who'd have guessed?' he muttered, loosening his shirt collar. 'He's never done this before, zooming back without a word.' His finger and thumb stroked the column of his throat in a nervous gesture. 'We're in trouble now. It's always bad news when he has that look about him.'

'Trouble?' she grated. 'We? You told me everything would be all right—he wouldn't mind, you said. "I run things, I have free rein," you said. "No problem," you said.'

'OK.' David held up a hand in supplication. 'So maybe I could have been a little carried away. It seemed like a good idea at the time. Anyway, you were the one who needed the money.'

Katherine scowled. 'You didn't have to remind me,' she told him, seething. 'Be practical, can't you? What are we going to do?'

'You're both going to come over to the house and do some explaining,' Rees Alton said from behind her in a voice that was much too quiet. Katherine gave a jittery start as he materialised by her side.

'I wish you wouldn't do that,' she complained with a touch of bitterness. 'Creeping up on people that way, you could give someone a heart attack. As it is you almost killed me earlier this afternoon, coming in on me without any warning. I might have fallen and broken my neck.'

'That would have been a great pity,' he said with cool precision. 'It would have taken away all the pleasure I'll have from doing it personally.'

She gasped and jumped away from him, drawing some small comfort from David's hard frame.

'Don't imagine your boyfriend will be any protection,' Rees said, his mouth curling nastily. 'You and I have a score to settle.'

'What's going on?' David asked, his tone bearing a heavy load of bewilderment. 'I don't understand any of this.'

'Shut up,' Rees told him. 'I'll get to you later.'

David's mouth closed abruptly and Katherine looked at him with irritation. Why didn't he stand up for himself?

To Rees she said resentfully, 'You lied to me. You said you weren't Alton.'

'I said you didn't know me,' he answered coldly. 'And that's true enough, isn't it, if you believed you could pull a fast one without repercussions? Did you imagine I'd accept your advice and stay out of your way so that you could turn my property into some kind of circus?'

'It wasn't like that——' she began.

'Will someone please tell me what's going on?' David demanded.

'Shut up,' Katherine said. 'I should never have listened to you in the first place.'

'Unless,' Rees said, in a glacial tone, 'you'd like me to tell the band to go home, you had both better accompany me to the house.'

There was a silence. Neither of them moved until Rees started towards the dais, and then David took off after him, saying quickly, 'We're with you, we're on our way.'

Katherine eyed him with disgust. All right, so she wanted to explain, and put matters right, but she was darned if she would let the man treat her as if she were a naughty schoolgirl and try to enforce his position with threats. She dug in her heels.

Rees turned, throwing a lancing glance in her direction, and David hastily made a grab for her hand. Propelling her towards the door, he muttered under his breath, 'Don't provoke him, you've no idea what you're dealing with.'

She smiled grimly. 'That goes for him, too,' she retorted, jerking her hand free.

'I mean it,' David warned. 'Just tread carefully, or I could end up in real hot water.'

They made their way through the grounds to the screen of silver birch trees that fronted the mellowed stone building, and if she hadn't been in such an aggravated mood Katherine might have stopped to admire Alton's house. As it was, she followed the taut-faced journalist through the wide porch and into a spacious, high-ceilinged lounge without pausing to give more than a fleeting recognition to the quiet elegance of his home.

He went over to a dark mahogany cabinet and pulled out a bottle of Scotch and a glass. Katherine's green eyes glittered, and he said tightly, 'Say one word, and you might not live to regret it.'

'That makes twice you've threatened me in the space of less than half an hour,' she said coolly. 'Do you have a problem handling these aggressive tendencies? Perhaps you should see someone about it, get some advice.'

'My advice to you is to sit down and mull over the catalogue of your own transgressions today,' he snarled. He poured a measure of the tawny liquid into his glass and took a large swallow. 'Maybe your conscience will come to the surface if you think about it long enough.'

She seated herself on a low couch, adjusting her skirt as she slid one slender leg over the other. He watched the action and took another pull at his drink.

David began uncomfortably, 'Look, I realise you need some kind of explanation here——'

'Oh, we have managed an agreement of sorts, then?' Rees's sarcastic comment made David wince.

'We hadn't intended that you would come back to find all this going on——' the latter tried to explain.

'I believe I had already worked that out for myself.' He shot a withering look at Katherine, and put his glass down with a clatter on to an onyx table. 'You decided that my coming home would be an inconvenience and then you programmed this vindictive blonde to maim me for life so that you could go ahead with your shindig. I can tell you, being under fire was nothing in comparison to what I have had to endure in the last few hours.'

David's jaw hung open. 'Vindictive blonde? Katherine?' He shook his head, a bemused expression on his face. 'I don't understand.'

'Katherine?' Rees tried out the syllables. 'Well, I suppose it's something to at least know the name of your persecutor.'

Katherine moistened her lower lip with the tip of her tongue. Slowly she said, 'I can understand that you've been under a considerable strain, and might be feeling a little fractious, but how on earth can you lay those charges at David's door? He didn't know that you were on your way back.'

'Of course he knew,' Rees bit out. 'I phoned this morning to say that I'd been pulled out at short notice, and that as soon as I'd called in on Sam I'd be on my way home. That must have given you plenty of time to get to work on your plan.' He viewed her with distaste. 'When did he phone the news to you? After I left Sam's? Lucky for you that you knew where I was headed.'

Sharp little needles of ice chased across Katherine's flesh as she turned her gaze on David. There was a stricken look about him, his face growing pale.

'The Ansaphone,' he managed. 'I thought there was a strange hissing sound on the tape when I checked it, but it's been working all right this afternoon. I didn't know—how could I have known?' His tone was almost a plea and she groaned inwardly, her lashes flickering down over her cheekbones.

'How very convenient,' Rees said, his mouth making a hard line. 'The phone went wrong just as I put through my call. But it's immaterial, anyway. I don't expect to have my land turned into a carnival site. If I had wanted that, I'd have employed a co-ordinator of festivities instead of an estate manager.'

Katherine asserted, 'David isn't to blame; there were reasons—I'm certain he thought that in normal circumstances you wouldn't object, but of course you've been in some hazardous situations lately and that's bound to give you a different perspective on things. Perhaps you'll feel better about it all after a good night's sleep.'

There was a sharp edge to his voice. 'Don't patronise me,' he said. 'And don't waste time trying to defend your boyfriend. He's well capable of doing that for himself. He doesn't need to hide behind a woman's skirts.'

'But I'm the one at fault. You have to listen to me.'

'I'm already aware of your part in it. You did everything in your power to keep me away, and you were very clever how you went about it. I didn't suspect for an instant.' A muscle flicked in his jaw. 'I have to give you ten out of ten for ingenuity and perseverance, not to mention sadism. Not content with throwing my keys into the nearest sewer inlet, you thought you could get me to book myself into a hotel for the night. When that didn't work you made sure I was involved for several hours in a publicity stunt.'

'I did no such thing,' Katherine exploded with indignation. 'A handful of people asked for your autograph. How does that constitute a Press conference all of a sudden?'

'So you admit you phoned the Press?'

'Phoned the——? Of course I didn't. Are you sure that spending all these months in foreign climes isn't affecting you? Ought you to see a doctor?'

'Somebody called them out,' he replied abruptly. 'I'm not going to argue the issue with you.

The fact is that I arrived back despite all the harassments. What is not clear,' he added, turning to David, 'is why you felt you had to make cash on the side—an activity which I believe is mentioned in one of the clauses in your contract. Don't I pay you enough?'

'It wasn't for David,' Katherine put in. 'It was for me. I wanted the money.'

His brows rose. 'Whatever for, I wonder? Had you run out of thumbscrews?'

She sucked in a sharp breath, and chose to ignore the remark. 'I needed funds to help out with the animal refuge that I'm involved with. The dance was a way of easing things a bit.'

Quite pleasantly Rees said, 'Refuge? May I ask where this refuge is sited?'

'Well—uh——' She paused. 'You see, I rent the Beech Wood cottage. It's—uh—an ideal place, with all the—uh—woodland around.'

He was very still, and she held her breath.

'*Next door*,' he gritted, underlining each word with deadly emphasis. 'You're telling me that you're running an animal refuge on my boundary?'

Slowly she nodded.

'What kind of animals are they?'

She hesitated. 'On the whole they're...well, in fact, I suppose you could say...'

'What kind?'

'Wild,' she said, adding quickly, 'But they're no trouble really, they're quite harmless—well, mostly...'

A growl started up in Rees's throat. She heard it and edged back in her seat.

'I see it all,' he said with a snarl. 'I'm going to be overrun with rodents and vermin. It's not enough that I have a shrew for a neighbour; there's a whole zoo building up around me. Why don't you advertise, so that people know where to come? When you get a long enough queue you can start charging admission.'

'Aren't you being a bit melodramatic about this?' Katherine murmured. 'Couldn't you perhaps sleep on it?'

'Are you becoming obsessed with my sleeping habits as well as my drinking habits?' he rasped. Rounding on David, he said tautly, 'What possessed you to let her do as she pleased? Have you lost your mind? This is valuable land; we can't run the risk of predators running loose around it, let alone hordes of people tramping wherever they please.'

'I didn't see any harm,' David muttered. 'We put up rope barriers to contain the area where people could walk about. I didn't think you'd mind as long as it was well organised. It seemed like a good cause, and I wanted to help.'

Rees looked from him to Katherine, and back again. 'Persuasive, was she? What inducements did she hold out?' His eyes glittered over her slender shape. 'You're a fool, David.'

Stung, Katherine said heatedly, 'You've no right to slander me that way. David told you he wanted to help, and that's true. He's a decent, thoughtful man, and you've no business to put any other interpretation on his actions.'

'Oh, well done,' Rees applauded with a sneer. 'If I believed anything you said, you'd have me crying into my shirt. Tell me, why is he changing colour if it was all so innocent?'

Her eyes widened. The man was way off-beam. 'You're impossible,' she told him briskly. 'I suspect you've had a touch too much sun, otherwise you wouldn't be drawing conclusions like that. Unless, of course, you judge everyone by your own standards.'

His mouth tightened ominously, and it occurred to her that she might have gone too far. After all, basically they were in the wrong, and he had been through a lot over the last months. She didn't want to be responsible for pushing him over the edge. Somehow she would have to try to appease him.

'I can promise you,' she said, using a placatory tone, 'the animals won't bother you in any way. There's no chance of their getting out, especially now that the dance has brought in extra money for new cages and equipment.'

'You'd better hope that's true. You wouldn't want to be around if they ever escaped on to my property.'

Katherine opened her mouth to answer, but her words were lost in a shrill eruption of sound that burst in on them from outside. As one, they turned to the window, watching as the night sky was streaked with a blaze of colour, and a flash of eerie light filled the crevices of the room.

A spangled golden sunburst radiated over the dark velvet panoply of the heavens, followed swiftly by a shimmering display of silver rain falling to the ground. Rees was already on his way to the door as the piercing whine of a rocket accompanied its lightning passage across the softly glowing network of stars.

Katherine gathered her wits and went after him, picking her way carefully through the dark shadows of the trees. A phosphorescent glare momentarily lit her path and she stopped to get her bearings. Firecrackers exploded with spine-tingling ferocity against the throbbing beat of the music which emanated from the open doors of the barn.

Her ears were assaulted by an excited cacophony of squawking from what must have been a distant hen coop. To her right, she heard the terrified whinny of a horse, and the thud of hoofs pounding in agitated discordance against a hard surface. She turned in the direction of the stables, her throat closing in dismay as she listened to the anguished squeal of an animal in pain.

Rees was already in there, trying to quieten a half-crazed stallion. Cold with fear, Katherine watched as he manoeuvred to avoid the crashing hoofs and reach for the animal's mane with his hand, his voice all the while soothing, low and reassuring.

The chestnut thoroughbred snorted, his breathing laboured, nostrils flaring widely. Eventually the panicked lunges died away as he responded to Rees's quiet, positive tone, and the firm hand at his head. He allowed himself to be stroked gently.

David appeared at the door, and Rees said, 'Go and find who's responsible for the fireworks and put a stop to it. I'll check the other horses.'

It took him several minutes to look over the two other animals, who were trembling feverishly in their stalls. When he returned Katherine told him, 'This one has hurt himself. His leg is bleeding quite badly. He'll need treatment.' She looked around. 'He must have caught it on that wooden rail—it looks as though it has splintered with the force of his kicks.'

'It's hardly surprising. He was terrified out of his mind. It's a wonder he hasn't done himself more harm than that.' Rees knelt to look at the gashed leg. 'I'll have to get Digby out to look at this.' He glanced up as David came back, and said, 'Did you sort them out?'

David nodded. 'They were no trouble. Just some youths who got a bit high-spirited. They won't do it again.'

'You'd better stay with Zac while I go and phone.'

'There's no need to disturb Digby at this time of night,' Katherine put in quickly, laying a hand on his arm as he went to the door.

Rees brushed off the hand. 'I'll be the judge of what needs to be done.'

'But I can——'

'You're in my way, let me through.'

'She could help,' David told him. 'Katherine could fix him up in a jiffy.'

Rees's mouth made a grim line. 'I want a vet,' he said with biting scorn, 'not one of the gamekeeper's camp followers who fancies playing Florence Nightingale.'

Katherine's shoulders went back. Stiffly, and with great dignity, she told him, 'I am a fully qualified vet. I work with Digby, and I'm quite capable of seeing to the needs of this animal. If you could just wait while I get my bag from the cottage, I'll do whatever's necessary.'

Rees's eyes narrowed. 'You'd better be telling the truth.'

The man was an unpleasant, disagreeable boor. She muttered, coolly, 'If you'll excuse me, I'll get my things.'

If it weren't that his animal was in obvious distress she'd walk out on him right now and never give him the time of day. As it was, she'd make certain that as soon as she had attended to his horse she'd be on her way, and have nothing more to do with him.

With any luck, before too long, his TV company would have him winched out to an area more in keeping with his temperament—the North Pole, perhaps, to report on the worsening break in the ozone layer. If all went well, if the fates were with her, he'd have an argument with a crevasse and disappear from view. The picture that conjured up brightened her spirits considerably.

'I'll come with you,' David said hurriedly, following her out of the stall. 'You might need some help. It's pretty black out there.'

Her teeth were set grimly and she didn't answer him, but she felt his glance on her as they walked along the rough gravelled path.

'You mustn't let yourself get too upset by the things he said. It's not really personal, you know.'

She gave a harsh, choked laugh. 'He had me fooled, then. If that wasn't personal, I'd hate to be around when he made sure that it was.'

'What I mean is,' David muttered, 'it's not just you—I think it's most women that bring out the worst side of him. You shouldn't take it to heart.'

'You expect me to laugh off the fact that he treats me like some kind of prize floosie?' Her lips made a contemptuous line. 'You've got to be kidding. Why should I do that, when the man's nothing but a philanderer himself? He may not like women over-much, but he doesn't object when they serve a purpose, does he?' She remembered the devil's smile and scowled fiercely.

Her temper had not eased any by the time they returned to the stables, and she put her medical case down on the hard floor with a thud, before bending to look at the injured limb.

Glancing at his watch, David said, 'I'd better get back to the barn and wind things up over there. The band are due to finish in about ten minutes.'

He left them, and Katherine ran her fingers carefully over Zac's tendons. 'Move out of the way,' she told Rees curtly. 'I don't need you breathing down my neck while I work.'

His eyes sparked for an instant, but he stood to one side and watched while she examined the animal with swift efficiency.

'I'm giving him an injection to lessen any risk of infection,' she said, 'but he'll also need some antibiotic capsules. I can let you have a week's supply to begin with, and then we'll see how he goes.'

Handing him a small plastic tub, she snapped the lock on her bag and straightened up. 'If there's any problem, give us a ring at the surgery.'

Rees glanced at the label on the tub before sliding it into his pocket. 'You handled him well,' he admitted grudgingly. 'Zac's not an easy customer, but you seemed to know what you were doing.'

'I'm so glad there's some tiny thing I can do that meets with your approval,' she retorted tersely.

'What did you expect, after the way things have gone today? I haven't had a decent night's sleep in over a week, and I come back home to find music blaring and people swarming all over the place.'

He reached for the overhead light-switch and flicked it off as they went out into the cool night air. In the sudden darkness Katherine stumbled and he snagged her arm with his hand, preventing her fall.

She would have liked to shrug off his assistance but being unfamiliar with the layout of the grounds meant that moving around was a tricky business, and she had to rely on his surefooted path-finding or risk a broken ankle.

'If I had known you were coming back,' she said with a sigh, 'I'd have called it off. I was telling you the truth earlier—I didn't know until you walked into the barn. I never intended to disturb you in any way.'

He replied drily, 'You were on a loser, then. You'd disturb a saint.'

They approached the barn, where light spilled out into the surrounding area, and she dislodged his light grasp with a feeling of relief. The corners of his mouth made a derisive curve and she looked away, her cheeks flushing with warmth.

From the appearance of the almost empty room it was obvious that David had done his job. Most of the people were already making for the large double gates, marking the exit further along the drive, their light-hearted chatter filtering back along the pathway. Only a few remained, a couple of young girls who were helping David to stack chairs, and clear up debris, and a woman whom Katherine recognised as a local councillor.

She was talking to her husband, as they went in, but when she spotted Rees she came towards him, a smile creasing her face.

'Mr Alton!' she exclaimed. 'How wonderful to see you back in Fairoak at last. We all follow your reports on the television, you know. You're such a busy man—and that makes your show of public spirit this evening even more praiseworthy.'

For a second or two Rees looked blank, and Katherine used her hand to suppress a cough.

'I—that's very kind of you, Mrs Talbot,' he murmured. 'I'm not certain, though, that I merit such kudos——'

'You're too modest by far,' Mrs Talbot interrupted, putting up a hand to quiet him. 'It was a very thoughtful decision you made in allowing this dance to go ahead on your property. In fact, you've been so magnanimous, it makes me wonder whether I dare encroach on your generosity in another cause?'

Katherine spluttered again, and the older woman said, 'That's a nasty cough you have, my dear. I do hope it clears up soon.'

Catching Rees's dark-eyed appraisal, Katherine murmured huskily, 'Thank you, I'm sure it will.'

Rees said, 'What was it you wanted to ask, Mrs Talbot?'

Remembering her purpose, the woman gave a little gulp, her hands fluttering in an excited, fragmentary gesture. 'It was about our annual dog show,' she explained. 'It's a charity event that we're holding in a couple of weeks, and it would do so much for attendance if we could lend your name to the proceedings. Having a celebrity such as yourself making an appearance would practically guarantee the day's success.' She gazed at him with entreaty. 'Do say you'll agree. It's for the blind, you know.'

'I see.' It looked as though Rees was giving the idea some consideration, and Katherine wondered how he was going to get out of it without seeming churlish. It was a wonder he hadn't come out in a rash at the mere suggestion.

He glanced her way, and she made a determined effort to hide the cynical amusement that his discomfiture provoked in her.

'I think, Mrs Talbot,' he said slowly, 'I could only consider it under one condition.' His glinting dark eyes slid over Katherine, and she stiffened. 'I'd like Katherine to come along too. She could act as one of the judges.'

Katherine looked at him with barely concealed horror, her jaw dropping. How could she spend so much as a minute longer than necessary with that stiff-necked, self-opinionated monster? It was unbelievable that he could suggest such a thing. She clamped her lips together. He was doing this to get back at her.

'What a wonderful idea,' the councillor was saying. 'Of course; Miss Shaw would be just the person we need. That's settled, then—I'll get back to you with details. Thank you so much.'

A short time later she left with her husband, and Katherine turned to Rees with bubbling animosity. 'Why did you do that?' she demanded. 'I could be working that day, or have other plans, for all you know.'

'Cancel them,' he drawled lazily. 'It's all in a good cause—you'll feel better about it after a decent night's sleep.' His devilish blue-grey eyes mocked her, and she had to steel herself not to lash out at him.

He began to walk along the path towards the house, and she started after him.

'Look,' she said, picking her way cautiously over the gravel, 'I'm sorry you've had such a bad day, and I wish I could undo everything that's happened, but I can't. I know you're angry with me, and I wish you would see things in a different light. We can put all this behind us. All I can say is that I'll never bother you again, you have my promise. You won't know I'm around, believe me.'

'That won't work, for a start,' he pointed out with cool detachment. 'You'll be round here again tomorrow to take a look at Zac, won't you?'

She chewed her lip. 'Digby will take over,' she insisted. 'He usually deals with the larger animals.'

'I think not in this case,' he murmured. 'You started the treatment, I prefer you see it through to the end.' He slotted his key into the lock of his front door.

'Wait,' she muttered. 'You can't just leave me this way; I need to talk to you.'

'OK,' he said agreeably, pushing on the hard oak panelling so that the door opened into the large hall. 'I'm on my way to bed—would you care to join me?'

'Damn you, Rees Alton, you're an insolent swine.'

He laughed. 'Tell me something I've not heard. Do I take it that you're refusing my invitation?'

Her jaw clenched in impotent fury. 'You're so right,' she said through her teeth. 'That's one proposition that I'll never take up.'

His mouth shaped a fiendish curve. 'Never is a long time, you know. You should be careful about making such sweeping statements.' He pulled his keys from the door and pocketed them. 'I'll see you in the morning, Katherine.'

CHAPTER THREE

SUNLIGHT streamed in through the kitchen window, and Katherine felt its warm caress on her bare arms as she stared at the geranium plant on the sill. Bright crimson petals nodded at her sleepily, as if in reproach, and vaguely she recalled that she had been about to do something.

Water. That was it. She had meant to water the plant, before she had been side-tracked into clearing the table.

Her concentration had gone to pieces today, and it was all because of him, Rees Alton, and the unwelcome prospect of having to go round to his place some time this morning. Having him as a neighbour, living in such close proximity to her small cottage, was an unwelcome, unnerving reality. Since she had woken this morning her thoughts had done nothing but revolve around him, and it was distracting in the extreme. It was a good thing it was Sunday and Digby was doing the morning surgery. She was fit for nothing today.

The watering-can weighed heavily in her hand and absently she angled its spout over the plant. Creamy milk dripped on to the green leaves and splashed on to the soil and she stared at it in dismay.

Looking with disgust at the jug she was holding, she told herself that she could not go on like this. That man could not be allowed to interfere with her faculties this way. Replacing the milk jug in the fridge with a thump, she drew out the watering-can.

Last night he had taunted her, making his provocative suggestion in order to aggravate her, and he had succeeded well enough. Even now the memory of his casually thrown out invitation was enough to send a feverish heat pulsing beneath her skin. The trouble was, casual though his words had been, she was certain that they had not been idle. Simply, he had not bothered to wrap up his message; it was there loud and clear, and he made no apology for it.

Before she had turned away from him his eyes had held a gleaming promise that had made her toes curl. His body, long and lean, and fit, was sending out signals that had her pulses leaping. He wanted her, there was no doubt, and if she had pushed her luck, and gone into his house, it would have been like walking into the wolf's lair. He would have devoured her.

With a supreme effort she hauled back her wayward thoughts from the fiery brink to which they had led her. She didn't even like him—how ever could she have let her mind be enticed along that path?

It was obviously time that she pulled herself together and set to work on the list of things she had to do today. Perhaps she had better go over to his house as soon as she had seen to the animals—that way it would be over and done with, and she wouldn't have the prospect pulling at her nerves all day.

Guzzler, she discovered, a short time later, had spent the night killing his blanket and tossing his battered furry teddy bear around his pen.

'I suppose,' she said in amusement, 'you're not too busy to take a pull at this?' She held out the bottled feed to him, and he stopped nosing around the bushes long enough to trot over and climb into her arms. Watching him suck noisily at the teat, she reflected that he was the easiest of her charges to care for.

Fang was a different customer altogether, and she approached the yellow-brown ferret with more than a little caution.

'Hold still,' she admonished the wriggling bundle as she lifted him to inspect the wound on his belly. It was beginning to heal at last. 'You're not doing so badly,' she told him, dropping him carefully back into the hutch, where he made a dive for his drain-pipe burrow.

It took only a half hour to check over the other animals, and she realised with a qualm that she could no longer put off the visit to Alton's domain. She sighed heavily. She might as well face up to it.

When no one came to answer her ring at the front of the house, she decided to venture by the shrubbery. Perhaps he was around the back somewhere.

Rounding a corner, she saw that at the far end of the building glazed doors opened out on to a wide terrace, and she could hear voices coming from the room beyond.

'They broke in through the fence by the hen coop,' Rees was saying, his clear voice low and evenly modulated. 'It was probably the youths whom you spoke to last night—there's a heap of burnt-out fireworks scattered on the ground out there.'

'They won't come back,' David said. 'They wouldn't dare.'

'Even so, make sure the fence is repaired straight away. We don't want to encourage intruders.'

There was a pause, and Katherine heard a rustling sound like papers being moved about. 'Also, before you go——' it was Rees again '—I've had a letter from the tenants of Mill House, a complaint. Apparently you didn't make the annual survey of premises, and their request to have the heating system serviced hasn't been acted on. It appears there's a problem with the boiler.'

'I've been meaning to see it, but other things cropped up.' David's tone was defensive.

'It's almost two months overdue,' Rees pointed out.

'I didn't think it was as long as that,' David muttered, 'but anyway it's summertime; the system's not likely to be in use much yet.'

'I want it sorted out before the end of next week,' Rees said. 'Tenants have a right to decent conditions, the same as you and I.'

'I don't know that I can get to it so soon,' David prevaricated. 'There's still the lower meadow to be sorted out.'

Katherine's footsteps slowed. Maybe this wasn't the moment to butt in. David might not be too happy at the untimely intrusion, and she wondered whether she ought to retrace her steps and ring the front doorbell again. Then again, she could be waiting there all day.

Rees's voice had a steely edge to it. 'You'd better make sure that the work I've mentioned takes priority,' he advised him shortly, 'or you could be looking for another job. There have been too many things left undone before this. If it hadn't been that I took you on as a favour to an associate you'd have been out long ago. This is your final warning.'

Katherine came to a complete halt, indecision rooting her to the spot. She felt like an intruder, listening in to a private conversation, but she hadn't meant to stumble in on them. What was she to do? She didn't want to embarrass David by letting him know that she had heard.

She struggled with the problem for a moment. If she made as much noise as she could, they would think that she had only just arrived. Scuffling her feet on the paving stones, she called out, 'Is anyone there? Hello? Mr Alton?'

'The name is Rees,' he said, walking out on to the patio as she came up to open the doors.

'I've been ringing, but you didn't——' She broke off, her heart giving a strange jolt as she took in the sight of him.

Dressed in immaculate white linen trousers and a short-sleeved shirt, faintly striped in blue, there was an aura of powerful masculinity about him that took her breath away. His black hair was crisp and clean as if he had just showered, the short crop of waves gleaming with iridescent highlights. His square-cut jaw was firm, the hard angles of his face somehow different this morning, making him even more dangerously attractive than he had been before.

'You've shaved,' she blurted, and immediately wished that she had clamped a hand over her mouth. It was just that seeing him this way had come as a complete shock to her system and her mind had gone haywire.

He made a wry smile. 'It's something I do occasionally,' he said. 'Is it an improvement? Do I look less like a vagabond?'

She was flustered. 'I'm sorry, I didn't mean...'

'You most probably did, but we won't go into that now. Come on in.'

Taking her arm, he drew her into the room and indicated a chair by a dark oak table. Crockery and papers littered the surface and the tantalising smell of freshly ground coffee wafted across to tease her nostrils.

David looked up and smiled as she walked towards him. He was holding a mug in one hand and sifting through a pile of letters with the other.

'I'll move these out of your way,' he said, draining the contents of his mug, and sliding it on to the table. He didn't seem put out by his earlier conversation with his boss, and she concluded that he must be used to the vagaries of the other man's moods. He had probably put it down to nothing more than irritability after the nerve-racking months he had spent abroad and his troublesome homecoming. A sneaking quiver of guilt at her own involvement washed over her and she quickly suppressed it. Alton had been less than polite to her; in fact, he had been downright insulting, hadn't he?

'We've just been going over some estate matters,' Rees told her, and to David he said, 'Would you see to the things we discussed? We'll talk again later.'

'Leave it with me,' David affirmed, raising his hand in a farewell salute to Katherine as he went out.

She hadn't realised until now just how extensive Rees's interests and holdings must be. From the looks of things he didn't need to follow a career, and that made it all the more strange that he should choose to involve himself in such a dangerous and unsettling line of work.

His voice broke in on her thoughts. 'Would you like a coffee?' He lifted a finely crafted ceramic coffee-pot, and she sniffed appreciatively as he poured one for himself.

'Thanks.'

'I'm just about to have breakfast,' he said. 'Will you join me?'

'Breakfast?' She glanced at her watch and he looked at her balefully.

'I slept in late—is that another black mark? We'll just about cancel each other out at this rate. You can call it lunch if you like. Would you care for some?'

'I—I'd better not. I should get on. If I could just go over to the stables——'

He shook his head. 'Wait while I eat first.'

She tensed slightly, and his glance ran over her, taking in the slender cut of the jeans that moulded themselves faithfully to her hips, and the skimpy T-shirt that did nothing to disguise her curves. Fervently she wished that she had chosen to wear something else this morning, something voluminous and all-concealing.

His mouth quirked, his teeth showing white and even. 'Why don't you sit down? I promise I won't leap on you—not yet, anyway.'

A rush of heat invaded her cheeks. The man was insufferable, a demon bent on provoking her, but she wouldn't rise to his bait. He was waiting for her to refuse, just so that he could pounce again and make her squirm.

She sat down, scowling darkly as he began to fill his plate from a warming-dish.

'Help yourself,' he instructed her, pushing a rack of toast in her direction. 'There's bacon too, if you want it.'

She eyed the toast moodily. There was no way she wanted to share a table with him, but then again it seemed a long time now since breakfast, and if she was forced to wait while he tucked in...

Taking a slice from the rack, she buttered it, surreptitiously looking at him while she nibbled at one corner.

A smile tugged at his lips. 'You're getting the idea,' he murmured. 'Live dangerously. Eat with the devil.'

Her toast went down the wrong way, and she almost choked, her eyes watering. He couldn't know that she thought of him that way, could he? He wasn't a mind-reader, was he? Damn him for making her feel so uncertain and out of sync. It was just what she might have expected from someone like him. He couldn't resist the opportunity to make her feel ill at ease.

'Having problems?' he queried with fiendish humour, his fork poised over the meat dish. 'You shouldn't bite off more than you can chew, you know.'

'I'll remember that,' she muttered. She'd remember, too, that he was far more astute than she had given him credit for, and it wouldn't do to underestimate him. Lowering her eyelids, she sipped slowly at her coffee while she tried to recover her equilibrium. He rattled her, and it wasn't an experience she was used to. The sooner she finished what she had come to do and left here, the better she would feel.

After what seemed like an eternity, he pushed away his plate and said, 'If you're ready, we'll go and take a look at Zachary.'

He stood up, and came around the table towards her, and Katherine was taken aback by his tall, lean vitality. Refreshed after his meal, and a good night's sleep, he seemed to exude energy and strength, the subtle interplay of muscles distractingly evident beneath his shirt as he reached forward to draw back her chair.

She got to her feet. 'Have there been any problems overnight—any restlessness?'

He looked at her quizzically. 'In whom? Me, or the horse?'

Her breath hissed through her teeth and he laughed. She said tightly, 'Contrary to your egotistical imaginings, Mr Alton, I am most definitely not interested in your sleeping habits. The horse, however, is another matter entirely. He is a total innocent and deserves all the attention he can get.'

'Oh, come down off your pedestal, Miss Shaw. You sound like an affronted nun and I've hardly had time to tweak your habit yet.'

'Don't imagine that waiting around will give you the opportunity, will you?' she retorted. 'Or you'll find you're on the road to disillusionment.'

He nodded. 'I've travelled that way before, you know. But there are always bypasses. Shall we go?'

Leading the way out to the stables, he said, 'As far as I can tell, nothing untoward has happened to him since last night. I'd have called you before if I'd noticed anything. Apart from any other consideration he's a valuable animal. He's sired more than a few winners.'

She replied coolly, 'Perhaps you would rather call Digby in to look at him. After all, if you let me tamper with him, who knows what damage I might wreak?'

'An unlikely eventuality while I'm watching you, sweet Kate. Don't you realise that I have your number now? One false move and I'm ready.'

'I'm quaking in my shoes,' she muttered, and walked through to the stall where the magnificent chestnut snorted testily. For some reason he reminded her of his owner, and she regarded the animal with a wary eye.

'There's no sign of inflammation,' she pronounced a short while later. 'Everything seems to be going well so far.'

'That's good.' Rees went to the door, and she followed him, relieved that her job was done, and that there were no complications.

Outside, in glorious contrast to the dark interior of the stable, the sun beat down, and she put up a hand to shield her eyes as the overhead call of a gull turned her head skywards. Letting her medical bag slide to the floor by the wall, she followed the bird's swooping progress with her eyes and said quietly, 'I'd have thought we were too far inland for gulls.'

'It's the lake that draws them.'

'The lake—I'd forgotten; you mean the one above——?' She turned and collided with his long-limbed body. He towered over her and the fusion of soft, pliant curves against firm, hard-packed muscle shocked her to the core. She stumbled back against the sun-baked wall, and he seemed to move with her, so close that where the top few buttons of his shirt lay open she could see the fine pores of his bronzed skin, and the rugged line of his jaw was only a fraction away from contact with her lips. The notion brought with it a swift, engulfing wave of heat.

'The one above long meadow,' Rees said. 'You must have seen it?'

She shook her head, dry-mouthed, and thought dazedly how startling and unusual his eyes were, such an intense grey-blue that they seemed to change with the light.

Negligently, he leaned one hand, palm flat, against the wall, and Katherine breathed in his own subtle, evocative male scent. The intimacy of his body so near to her own and the warmth at her back combined in a way that dispelled coherent thought, her mind floating, adrift, as though, in some way, she had been mesmerised.

She knew a sudden primitive urge to reach out and touch him, to trail her fingers over the strong column of his neck and let them tangle with the silkiness of the hair at his nape. The blood seemed to throb inside her head, building up a crescendo of sound, and she wondered frantically how her thoughts could have taken such a wild and dizzying turn.

'How could I have seen the lake?' she asked, her voice oddly breathless. 'It's on your land. I've never been over there.'

The grey-blue eyes were lazily searching, and her heart stilled as she felt the slow burn of his gaze work its way along the vulnerable curve of her throat.

'That can be remedied,' he said softly, his glance sliding over her bare, gold-tinted arms, and her skin reacted as though he had brushed his fingers in a silken glide over her flesh. Yet he had not moved, and she stayed transfixed, the hot sun beating down on them, with no breath of wind to stir the air. It was the heat that brought on this madness, she told herself in desperation. It had to be insanity, the way her mind was behaving.

'You would like it,' he murmured, his voice low, slightly rough-edged. 'It's a beautiful place. I'll take you up there, while we still have the long, hot summer days, and you can lie in the grass among the speedwells and ox-eye daisies, and let the sun bathe you.'

She had stopped breathing. Somewhere, listening to his husky, compelling voice, she had forgotten to make her lungs work. Her green eyes skittered, and encountered his mouth, firm, mobile, attractive, and so much closer than she had imagined. A fierce, sweet ache pulled at her stomach as she stared. She was stunned by the power of the sensations that flooded through her, the staccato hammering of the pulse that beat in her throat, growing louder with every second.

Rees moved, but he was taking a step backwards, away from her, and then he turned, and Katherine blinked, shivering as though she had been deprived of sunlight. She stared bleakly at his broad back, the wide shoulders and lean hips, her mind unfocused until she, too, heard the sound, the tap of heels on concrete, and clarity came with shattering suddenness.

'Rees, darling, here you are. I've been looking everywhere for you. I was beginning to think you'd never get back from that interminable assignment. I've missed you so much.'

The woman was beautiful. Incredibly lovely. She had the kind of looks that men fought battles over: tawny eyes, huge in an exquisite heart-shaped face, her glossy black hair cut in a smooth, chic style that added piquancy to the delicate features. A figure that women the world over would envy.

Katherine stared in wide-eyed dismay as the woman walked towards Rees and laid her head on his chest. His arms closed around her.

'Hello, Alison,' he said.

'Tell me that you've missed me, too,' Alison demanded, her voice softly lilting.

'Of course.'

Rees held her away from him, and ran an assessing eye over her. 'How have things been with you? You look well. Is the publishing business still thriving?'

'Oh, work, work. Father thinks of nothing else. How long are you home for, Rees?'

'My plans are fluid at the moment.' He picked up the medical bag from the floor, and pushed home the bolt on the stable door.

Katherine wished uncomfortably that she could be somewhere else, anywhere but around these two. She was in the way. Sending Rees a meaningful glance, she indicated the bag, but he did not release it.

He said, 'Alison, have you met Katherine? She's one of our local vets—I'm indebted to her for giving Zac the once-over.'

'Oh, really.' Amber eyes turned her way, and Katherine saw that beneath the surface they held all the charm of a tigress. A tigress who was marking her prey. 'No,' Alison answered slowly. 'We haven't met before.'

Katherine was acutely conscious of her dishevelled appearance beside the model-girl perfection of the other woman. What had seemed a good idea this morning, when she had twisted her hair up into a precarious knot in order to keep the heat from her neck, did not appear so great right this moment. Unruly tendrils drifted down in wispy curls that refused to be controlled, and she was aware of a deepening flush of pink spreading across the bridge of her nose and along her cheekbones. She had been out in the sun too long, she told herself. It had nothing to do with Rees and the reckless meandering of her thoughts.

Heaven alone knew how she had let herself get into that kind of situation. The man was an obvious womaniser, ready to take up any opportunity that presented itself, and she had behaved like a complete idiot. She had to get a grip on herself. She couldn't afford to let her guard down, especially not with a man like him.

She directed another significant look towards the bag, and Rees said, 'Let's go back to the house and get some cool drinks.'

'If I could just have my bag, I'll be on my way,' Katherine muttered, but he wasn't listening. Alison slipped a hand around his arm, as they started off along the path, her long, manicured fingernails splayed out possessively over his tough sinews.

Katherine's glance went regretfully to her own short pink-tipped nails before she rammed them into the pockets of her jeans.

'If you've no particular plans at the moment,' Alison was saying, 'why don't you come to London and spend a few days with us? We're having open house to celebrate the new deal Father's made. You know he would love to have you stay, and you did promise last time...'

'I'm supposed to be seeing James Carlyle in a day or so...'

'Well, there you are. He's one of the people already invited; you can kill two birds with one stone. Say you'll come.'

Rees nodded thoughtfully. 'You've twisted my arm,' he said, and Alison treated him to a smile, her wide, full mouth curving sensuously.

They had arrived back at the house, and Katherine decided that enough was enough. She did not want to stay and watch them fawning over one another.

David had been right about Rees's attitude to women. He used them, like an amusement to be taken up or discarded at a whim. Of course it did not bother her what Rees did, or who he did it with, for that matter. She had far too much to fill her life than to be concerned about the rakish activities of a first-class flirt. It was bad enough that he lived next door, without having to act as an onlooker to his sexual conquests as well.

'I need my bag,' she told him crisply, and he looked down at the brown leather case in his hand as if he had never seen it before.

'Aren't you coming in for an iced drink? You look as though you could do with one.'

Her cheeks felt hot under his scrutiny. 'Don't trouble yourself,' she said. 'I have things I need to get on with.'

'Like checking the locks in the rodents' quarters?' He handed her the case. 'I'd hate to come back a second time and find my land overrun with another kind of visitor.'

'You needn't worry about that,' she replied tautly. 'I can assure you that nothing and no one from Beechwood Cottage will cause you the least disturbance.'

He smiled drily. 'Promises, promises.'

CHAPTER FOUR

'DOES Rees know that you have this sideline going?' Katherine looked up from the rose that she was de-thorning, and rubbed at the ache in the middle of her spine. She had been bending over for too long.

David shrugged. 'He wants rose-beds in this part of the estate, and that's what he has. I don't see any problem. Besides, while I'm living here this particular area is attached to my cottage. I can do as I like with it.'

Katherine's gaze drifted to the acreage of shrub roses that was not part of David's holding, but she didn't push the issue. She said mildly, 'This is more in the nature of an experimental exercise, isn't it? If you were successful and managed to create the perfect bloom, wouldn't it mean that you'd need to develop it further, buy land of your own?'

'That's all in the future,' David replied irritably. 'I'll cross that bridge when I come to it.'

'I just hope that Rees doesn't find out and put a spanner in your works.' She stretched, cautiously testing over-worked muscles. Somewhere in the distance a horse snorted.

'Haven't we done enough for now?' she asked. 'The light's fading fast, and anyway I'm beginning to feel hungry—I think someone from one of the cottages must have lit a barbecue. I can smell the smoke on the air, can't you?'

David mumbled something in reply, his attention on the rose in front of him, and Katherine wandered over to sit thankfully on the overturned tub that served as a makeshift seat.

Rees had returned home a couple of hours ago, David had told her. He had seen the car turn in on the drive. Katherine's fingers clenched on her bare legs, and she hurriedly thrust them into the pockets of her shorts. Although Rees had prolonged his stay in London by a day or so it appeared that he could no longer put off the matters that needed his attention back here. No doubt that would sour his mood.

The prospect of meeting up with him again filled her with unease. That last morning had been a total mistake, an aberration, and she couldn't imagine what had induced her to behave in such an irrational way. It made her go hot all over even to think about it. She had almost imagined that he would... Her mind hazed. Another few minutes and she might have made a complete idiot of herself. She gave a shudder. It had been the sun that did it; that was how she had been enticed into losing her head. A form of heatstroke, that was it.

After all, there was no way that she wanted any kind of involvement with that man. He was altogether too... male... too sure of himself and the attraction he held for women. Just look at the way his girlfriend had been all over him. There had been keep-off signs flying around like confetti, and if he had been at all aware of it he probably found it highly amusing.

Well, she wouldn't be caught out again. She'd be on her guard from now on, and besides, with Alison on the scene, the situation wouldn't arise another time, would it? They were well suited, that was for sure—she with her classy good looks and background, he with his wealth and authority.

If only there was some way she could avoid him—but it wasn't going to be possible, was it? There was still the dog show to contend with in a couple of days. He hadn't even made an objection when he had learned that it was being held close to his land, up by the long meadow.

The whinny of a horse cut across her thoughts, and she drew in a deep breath. It was time to go back to the cottage. She would have a shower and an early night, perhaps. For some reason she hadn't been sleeping well just lately, and the strain was beginning to tell on her.

Strange that the horses were so restless this evening. It could be the barbecue upsetting them, she supposed. The smoke was certainly heavier on the air than usual. She frowned, looking towards the horizon, and then jumped up in alarm. The tub fell on to its side.

'David, there's something wrong. Over by the stables; come on. Hurry.'

She didn't wait to see whether he was following her. She was already running, heading for the cobble-stone yard where the thick pall of sombre grey hung overhead and the shrill animal sounds snagged at her heart.

At the entrance to the brick and timber building she was forced to a horrified halt. Everything was black, smoke swirling around in every crevice and catching at her throat with acrid, choking fingers. The horses were screaming in panic, and she wished that she was not so hopelessly blind, that the ominous dark curtain would melt away and she could see to get to the stalls.

The air rasped in her lungs, and she covered her nose and mouth with her hand and knelt down, feeling her way across the hard floor with fingers that trembled. David ran up to the door and she heard his swift intake of breath.

'Go and ring the fire brigade,' she called. 'Quickly.'

He ran, and she resumed her inch by inch crawl over the cold surface until her shoulder banged against a wall of wood and she grazed her knee on a post. She pulled herself up to feel for the metal ring that held the gate in place, brushing her arm over eyes that smarted from the insidious invasion of smoke.

From the side of the building came the crackle of wood, and she turned her head to see orange and yellow flames licking at the timbers by the far wall. There was a spitting and the hiss of air as the fire took hold and the main beam caught alight, and she still had not found the wretched piece of iron she was searching for. She felt the cold tears of despair trickle down her cheeks. She had to find it—soon.

Heat from the wall of flame scorched her back as her fingers encountered the rigid bar, and she tugged, trying to lift it. Nothing happened and she almost wept aloud. It couldn't be stuck. Not now; it had to come free.

Footsteps, swift and heavy, sounded in the background. A glowing timber snapped overhead, and there was the tormented clattering of hoofs as the horses arched and plunged within the stalls. Amber light juddered over the brickwork, throwing into sharp focus the rolling, petrified eyes of the huge chestnut thoroughbred, his ears and mane thrown back in stark terror.

'Get out of there.' The male voice cracked across the building and she ignored it. Somehow she had to release the animals before the heat became too fierce, before the——

'Katherine, do as you're told. Get back. The roof's about to fall in.'

'No, we have to get them out, we can't leave them.'

'Dammit woman, listen to me——'

Rees made a grab for her hand and she pushed him away. His arms snaked around her waist and she hit out at him, using her elbows, her legs, anything that would make him let go. Her feet connected with his shin bone, yet still he clung on, dragging her away, and she swung at him with her fists. Taking avoiding action, he moved his head fast, and a post crashed down and caught him a glancing blow on the temple. Momentarily he reeled, his eyes blank, unseeing, and at last his hold on her slipped.

Katherine stared at him, appalled and uncertain, then saw with relief that he was still standing. Turning back towards the stall, she had almost made it, when his hard fingers locked in her shirt and the sound of material ripping mingled with the roaring of the fire in her ears as she struggled to get away. She caught a glimpse of his grim expression, the strong lines of his face tough and uncompromising, in the brief seconds before she was lifted, slung over his shoulder and left to pound furiously at his back as he headed for the door.

'Hold on to her.' He thrust her in a heap at David's feet, and went back into the inferno.

Shakily she stood up and looked fearfully towards the gates of hell which had swallowed him up. How could the fire have taken hold so quickly? It had seemed as if such a short space of time had passed, but now it was consuming everything in its path with devastating voracity.

'I can't stay here and do nothing,' she said, her voice anguished, her eyes pleading, and David stared at her with indecision. 'We have to do something,' she cried. 'We can't leave him to do it alone.'

'Here,' he muttered, thrusting an extinguisher into her hands. 'Keep well back and aim carefully. I'll use the other one. I don't suppose it'll do much good, but it might help a bit.'

They worked together, concentrating their efforts on the pathway from the stalls to the cobbled yard, and while she waited for the sound of Rees's reappearance the tension inside her tightened like the winding of a huge screw. Each time he went back into that place of Furies the muscles of her stomach clenched in fierce apprehension, and it was only when he finally emerged, soot-blackened and coughing, leading out the last of the horses, that Katherine felt the gripping bands snap inside her. He seemed to be unharmed, and her heart contracted painfully as she watched him walk out of the building. He did not speak, but there was something about him that made her shiver, something in the rigid, straight-backed way he moved, in the steel-grey glitter of eyes that stared at her from a face that was carved out of granite.

There was nothing they could do to prevent the destruction of the stables. It had all happened too swiftly, and they stood by in silence as the searing flames reduced the building to nothing more than a burnt-out shell.

The fire brigade arrived and took over, and when it was all finished, the animals had been settled as best they could, and there was nothing more to be done, Katherine slowly followed the two men back to the house.

Once they had assembled in the brightly lit lounge she could see that there was a livid gash across Rees's forehead and temple. Subdued, she said, 'That cut needs looking at. Do you have a first-aid box handy?'

'There'll be time enough for that later.' His tone was clipped, and he directed an angry glare towards David. 'Right now there are other, more important matters that concern me. Like, for instance, how the fire was started in the first place. Any ideas, David?'

'I don't know.' The younger man shifted uneasily. 'Everything was fine when I checked earlier this evening.'

'Was it? I'm sure if you tried very hard you could come up with some factor that might have a bearing on the situation.' The cold metallic glitter of Rees's eyes cut into his employee with the deadly precision of a knife.

David shook his head, his expression blank. 'I've no idea.'

'No? Then I'll tell you, shall I? While we were arranging new quarters for the horses I took a quick look around. The first thing I noticed was a hole in the fence that hadn't been repaired, and the second thing that caught my eye was a scattering of dead fireworks around the back of the stable block. It wouldn't have taken more than a few stray sparks to set the hay smouldering, would it?'

'I was going to pick up a fence panel at the weekend——'

'In the meantime I'm faced with a total rebuilding job. I imagine you thought the horses could be replaced just as easily?' There was suppressed fury in the sharp-edged words, and Katherine flinched. Why hadn't David carried out Rees's instructions?

'Of course not,' David said. 'I didn't think——'

'That's just the trouble, isn't it? You didn't think at all. The matter was no more than a passing interest to you.' Rees's fist slammed down on to the oak sideboard with a violence that made the wood reverberate, and Katherine bit into the soft inner flesh of her lip.

'The animals were OK, though,' David said with an attempt at conciliation. 'We discovered what was happening in time.'

'We?' Rees snarled the word, and Katherine read the storm building up behind the glitter of his eyes and wished that David had kept quiet. Anything that he said was almost certain to add to the rage that was rapidly gathering momentum. 'Why was Katherine involved at all?'

'I—— She was with me when she saw the smoke and raised the alarm.'

Rees's lips flattened against his teeth. 'I see. You were together. Am I supposed to be thankful that you were able to cool your ardour long enough to sort out this little problem? Let me tell you, I am not. I gave you specific orders regarding the maintenance of this estate, and you have not carried them out. Therefore as from this moment you have one month's notice to quit.'

David gasped. 'But the fire wasn't my fault. It was an accident.'

'What happened tonight is only secondary to what went on, or did not go on, before. If you had repaired the fence as I requested, we might not have had unwelcome visitors. It's not a question I'm prepared to discuss.'

'But I'll see to it this weekend—it's all in hand.'

'You're too late,' Rees said stonily. 'You threw away your last chance and that's an end to it. In the morning we'll talk over the remainder of your duties for the next four weeks. Goodnight, David.'

'But——'

'Goodnight.'

David looked as though he had been pole-axed, disbelief etched with harsh clarity into his features. He moved, swaying slightly, and Katherine stared, stricken, after his retreating figure. Her hand stole to her throat. She had known that he had his faults, but his guilt, surely, had only been in his immaturity, his reckless, devil-may-care attitude to life.

She turned to follow him, and Rees said, 'Wait. I want to talk to you.'

Her green eyes lifted, dazedly searching his face.

'It appears I have you to thank for preventing what could have been a catastrophe.'

'I don't want your thanks.'

'Nevertheless, I'm in your debt. I'd like to repay you in some way, if that's possible.'

'You could think again about David,' she said. 'You were too hard on him. You were angry with him, and that's understandable—it's been a bad night. But you went straight for the jugular and pinned everything on him, and it isn't fair. He's in shock——'

'What about the rest of us?' Rees queried dismissively. 'None of this would have happened if it hadn't been for his thoughtlessness. It seems to me that he has too many other things on his mind these days. He isn't concentrating on what should be of prime importance.'

Katherine's thoughts veered to David's interest in horticulture and his concentration on the shrubs he was developing, but Rees couldn't know about that, could he? Hesitantly she asked, 'What do you mean?'

'Isn't it obvious? His involvement with you is blotting everything else from his mind. Why else would he neglect to cover even the basic essentials of his job?'

'That isn't true,' she argued hotly. 'You're making it up to justify your actions.'

'I don't need to do that. Especially not to you.'

She felt her skin pale. No. She was nothing—less than nothing—in his eyes. To a man like him her appeal lay only in the fact that she was a woman, and even that had been merely a temporary diversion while he was separated from his girlfriend. He thought of her as little more than an irritant, a troublemaker who, from the looks of things, had the annoying habit of distracting his staff.

Weariness washed over her. It must be the aftermath, the release of all the pent-up emotions that left her feeling so desolate, as empty as that burned-out building. As if it would wipe out the exhaustion she was feeling she rubbed the back of her hand across her cheek, and then stared blankly at the black smuts left on her fingers.

Rees had moved. She heard the clink of glass, and then he came back to her and handed her a small crystal goblet.

'Drink that,' he said. 'You look as though you could do with it.'

She sniffed the amber liquid. 'Brandy,' she muttered. 'I don't like——'

'It will put some colour back in your cheeks,' he cut in impatiently. 'Don't think about it, just get it down in one swallow.'

His grey-blue eyes skimmed over her in swift appraisal, and all at once she was humiliatingly conscious of the way she must look. She was a mess, dirty and bedraggled, her face smudged with soot and smoke, her shirt in tatters so that one grimy shoulder lay as bare to his glance as her long, grazed and charcoal-streaked legs.

With as much dignity as she could muster she attempted to pull the ragged garment together with her free hand. Then, with slow deliberation, she placed the glass firmly on the table.

'I don't need your particular anodyne, Mr Alton,' she said shakily, 'and if you'll excuse me I have to go now. I have a surgery to run in the morning.'

A clear blue sky and a brilliant golden sun heralded the day of the dog show, and Katherine viewed both with mixed feelings. At any other time she would have welcomed such a glorious late summer day, but the knowledge that she would be sharing it with Rees was making her nervous and edgy. There was no way he was going to let her opt out of it; he had made that quite clear.

David said, 'I wish you didn't have to go to this event today. I could do with a friend right now.' He looked dejected, thoroughly miserable, and she wished there was something she could say that would help him.

'Why don't you come along?' she suggested, but he shook his head.

'He'll be there. I'd rather keep out of the way. Can't you make an excuse and stay home?'

'No, people are expecting me to be there.' She glanced at the local paper, lying open on the kitchen table. 'You could look down the situations vacant columns,' she said. 'There might be just the job you've always wanted.'

His mouth turned down at the corners. 'It isn't only the job that's the problem,' he muttered. 'I've lost the house as well.'

She frowned. 'I don't understand.'

'The house goes with the job, so in a very short while I shall have nowhere to live, as well as being unemployed. I don't know what I'm going to do. If there was just a chance that he would change his mind—I didn't expect him to take such an entrenched position. It wasn't as if I wasn't going to see to the fence—it was just that the roses had to be dealt with straight away.'

Katherine studied him unhappily. 'I hadn't realised that it meant your home as well. I wish there was something I could do——'

A rap on the door made a sharp intrusion into her thoughts, and she was still frowning as she went over to open it.

'Hello, Katherine.' Rees walked into the room as she stood to one side, his glance going to David. Under that cold, hard scrutiny David got hurriedly to his feet.

'I have to go,' he mumbled. 'I'll see you later, Katherine.'

She nodded, and watched him leave. Turning back to Rees, she saw that he was dressed for the occasion—casual, yet smart, his shirt open at the neck, fawn-coloured trousers teamed with a matching light jacket. He looked good, though she hated to admit it to herself. Only the dark bruising across his forehead marred his appearance, and served as a reminder of that fateful night.

'Are you ready?' His glance went to the slim gold watch on his wrist. 'The thing starts in half an hour.'

Picking up her bag, Katherine followed him out, locking the door behind her, and they turned to walk along the footpath towards the long meadow.

'How are the horses now? Have they settled down?'

'They don't appear to have suffered any lasting harm, thank heavens. Digby checked them over and said they'd probably take a week or two to get over the effects of all the smoke that they'd inhaled, but otherwise they seem to be OK.' He frowned. 'I'd expected you to call round.'

'I was busy with surgery,' she said. He didn't have to know that she had asked Digby to go in her stead.

Rees shot her a thoughtful look, and she went on quickly, 'You did well to get them all out in time. I didn't think it would be possible.'

'But you were going to try it all the same. You showed a remarkable amount of courage, Katherine.'

She shifted uncomfortably, averting her eyes from his assessing gaze. 'I wasn't scared. The danger didn't really get through to me until I stood back and watched you go in there.'

For a moment she was silent, deep in thought as she walked beside him along the rough path. Then, with a slight hesitation, she asked, 'Is that what it's like for you, most of the time, in your work? I mean the nervous tension—the fear, never quite knowing what's going to happen?'

His shoulders moved dismissively. 'Sometimes it can get a little hairy,' he admitted. 'But more usually it's a question of waiting around in hotels with other journalists until something comes along, and then we're all scrabbling for the phones at the same time.'

She suspected that he was deliberately making light of it. Some of the news bulletins she had watched had been enough to make her wonder what kind of man would choose to put himself in those danger zones when he might just as easily be sitting behind a news desk.

'When are you likely to be called away again?' she ventured. 'Do you have another assignment lined up?'

His mouth quirked. 'Are you anxious to be rid of me?'

Her colour rose faintly. 'How did you guess?' she murmured, and his grin widened.

'Shame on you—I've only just arrived home. I haven't had a vacation in a long time, so I'm going to make the most of this one. Sorry if that isn't what you wanted to hear.' He gave her a sidelong glance. 'Though I must say, so far it hasn't turned out quite as I had expected.'

She chewed pensively on her lower lip. As holidays went, this one had obviously had more than its share of set-backs, and her own involvement in them couldn't be discounted.

'Tell me about you and David,' he commanded, and she lost her footing and stumbled on a loose stone. He caught her hand, helping her to steady herself, and as soon as she had recovered she tugged it free.

'Why?'

'Because I'm curious.'

Katherine shrugged. 'I thought, from your comments, that you already knew everything there is to know about us.'

'Do I?'

She pressed her lips together. 'You've certainly made enough assumptions so far.'

'I'm asking you now.'

They turned in at the entrance to the field where a number of marquees and side-stalls had been set up, and she said, 'We've been friends for some time. Perhaps I understand him a little better than you do: he doesn't mean to appear casual about things—he can become very immersed and enthusiastic about something that interests him.'

Rees eyed the judges' dais and cluster of microphones and said grimly, 'It's a pity he wasn't more enthusiastic about his job.'

'I'm sure he is,' Katherine put in hastily. 'There must have been reasons for the delay with the fence—if you would only let him have one more chance I'm sure he's learned a lesson. He isn't likely to falter again.'

'He should have thought of that before and sorted himself out.'

'But to lose his house——'

'You're too soft.' He said it with a scornful slant to his mouth. 'He's not an infant to be protected, he's a grown man.'

'And you're an unfeeling, hard-bitten——'

She would have said more, but their arrival at the show had been noticed, and Rees was immediately surrounded by admiring fans, and a small group of committee members who urged him to take his place on the covered stand.

Their brief altercation might never have taken place. He made a delightful and charming speech, which entertained his audience and made them laugh, before he declared the show open. After that Katherine was kept too busy, studying the assembled pets and bestowing rosettes and trophies, to have time to dwell on her grievances.

Rees mingled with the crowd, chatting with young and old alike, but he was never so far away that she could not be aware of him. She stared at him abstractedly. People liked Rees Alton, that was clear. They flocked around him and warmed to him, blossoming under his attention. For no reason at all she felt a sudden, aching pang of loss.

High in the cloudless sky the sun blazed down like a molten orb, dazzling to look at, and bathing everything with its powerful rays. The afternoon was going well, and the charity's funds were likely to be swollen by a record attendance and the willingness of the easygoing crowd to spend their money at the stalls. They were relaxed, enjoying the lazy heat of the afternoon, applauding the judges' selections.

Katherine bestowed the last rosette with a smile for the sleek Afghan and its owner, and wondered why it was that people and their pets often seemed so alike. She lifted the honey-toned hair from the nape of her neck with a sigh, and thought for the hundredth time what a fool she was not to have pinned it up out of the way. The sun was merciless, and she was growing hotter by the minute. Her throat was parched. Surely it was time that they could leave.

Rees appeared at her side as though the mere thought had conjured him up. He held out a tall, frosted glass to her and she viewed it with relieved anticipation.

'You're not going to refuse this one, are you?' he said, withdrawing it momentarily, and for a second her jaw dropped. Her mouth was as dry as sand. She might faint from dehydration.

'It's a perfectly innocent fruit juice,' he murmured, lifting the glass and inspecting it carefully. 'Very cold, and delicious, I can guarantee. But perhaps you're not thirsty?' He half turned, taking a few steps away from her, and her nerves leapt into twitchy action.

'I am...I am,' she said huskily, reaching for the tumbler before he could make it do a disappearing act. 'Thanks.' She swallowed greedily, not pausing until she had drained the contents. She wasn't taking any chances.

He grinned and she pulled a face at him. 'That was a low trick,' she complained.

'It was worth it, though, just to see your expression.' He looked around at the slowly disappearing crowd, watching the people as they led their dogs towards the flag-festooned exit. 'Would you really have liked to take that St Bernard home with you?'

'From the way he had his paws planted on my skirt I was beginning to think that I wouldn't have much choice, to be honest,' she laughed. 'Though I do have a sneaking preference for large dogs. I've often thought about getting one.'

Rees cast a considering glance over her. 'Hmm. For protection, I suppose. Living alone, a dog could be the ideal substitute.'

'Substitute? For a man who would take care of me, you mean?' Katherine eyed him scathingly. 'I don't need anyone, thank you. I'm perfectly capable of looking after myself.' Her lips clamped firmly together.

'You don't have to tell me that. I've been on the receiving end, remember?' His smile was rueful. 'I'm not sure which would be more dangerous—when you're really concentrating, or when you're only giving the matter half your attention.'

She scowled and refused to allow her gaze to stray to the reddened weal across his forehead. If he would persist in getting in the way, that was his own fault. Why did she have to be constantly plagued by guilt?

They walked back towards the marquee that served as a bar, and replaced her glass on the counter, before heading out into the sunshine once more. Sliding an arm around her waist, Rees drew her out of the path of a stall-holder who was intent on steering his rail of clothes towards the rear of his van.

'I believe we could slip away now,' he murmured. 'Everything's about cleared up, and all the owners have gone away happy.'

She nodded distractedly. The touch of his hand, palm flat, the long fingers resting lightly against the thin cotton of her blouse, was having an unnerving effect on her senses. To him, it was just a perfectly natural gesture, but it had had the effect of sending Katherine's blood-pressure soaring rapidly to danger level. Even her heart was pounding like a steam engine. It was crazy. What on earth was the matter with her? Why did she have to react with such devastating intensity to his every move? She would have to steel herself against her own weakness if she was to survive.

Breathing deeply, she tried to shake away the silken web that had descended like a gossamer cloud over her mind. They had skirted the hawthorn that edged the field, and now she could see that they were approaching a stile.

'This isn't the way back,' she said, puzzled, her eyes on the distant horizon.

'It's a short cut. Besides, I want to show you the lake.'

'But——'

'Come on, it'll be cooler by the water.' He took her hand and led her through a spinney to a grassy clearing where a crop of ancient and gnarled trees surrounded a glassy expanse of water. Golden-centred lilies opened delicate white blooms to the sunlight, broad green leaves floating on the surface of the lake, and rippling gently with the flow of a small weir. Flecks of white foam darted at the base of the fall, mother-of-pearl glistening in the filtered rays of the sun.

Katherine stood very still, absorbing the tranquillity of the scene.

'It's beautiful,' she whispered. 'A jewel, like an island of serenity tucked away from the rest of the world.'

He nodded. 'That's how I would have described it,' he said quietly.

She stared in fascination at a huge twisted old tree, its branches sweeping down towards the ground, arcing across the brown earth. Moving slowly, she walked towards it, and paused to run her fingers over the roughened bark.

'Why don't you use it as a seat? It's been here for generations and I can vouch that it's rock-solid.'

The suggestion appealed to her. A low branch spread horizontally, like a hammock, and she hitched herself up on to it, stretching out her legs, her head and spine resting against the sloping curve. Leaning back, she idly surveyed the scene. From her vantage-point she could see the damselflies darting on the water, and watch the tiny wading birds searching for food over by the far bank.

Her eyelids drooped, and she let herself absorb the pure calm of this little haven, her body relaxed and filled with a heavenly languor. Only the hum of insects and the soft burbling of water disturbed the air.

'It's so peaceful,' she breathed.

'I thought you would like to see it.' Rees spoke softly, and she opened her eyes to find his smoke-blue glance dwelling on her.

Suddenly she remembered his words about lying among the ox-eye daisies and speedwells and she looked away, a faint flush running along her cheekbones.

'Look,' she said, seeking a distraction, 'there's a mallard, poking about in the water.'

He followed the direction of her pointing finger. 'The rest of the family won't be far away—we've had some new additions since I was here last.'

He joined her, sitting on the far end of her branch, leaning back against the huge trunk of the tree. 'I like to come here,' he said. 'It was one of the features that influenced me when I bought the estate.'

Lazily, she lifted a brow. 'Not the tenancies or——' she was going to say stables, but thought better of it at the last moment '—other lucrative aspects?'

His mouth tilted at the corners, and she had the uncomfortable feeling that he knew very well what she had omitted, but he said, 'They were considerations, of course, but other estates would have provided similar. I think it was this place that swayed me most of all.' He stared musingly at the lake. 'When I'm away it's good to think that it's here, waiting for me to come home to it.'

For a moment Katherine's mind wandered, and she pictured him in some far-off country, away from his family and friends, with the sound of gunfire in the background and his mind switching for solace to this secluded, peaceful backwater. It was an unbearably painful thought, and she drew in a deep, aching breath.

Straightening, she told him, 'I'm glad you have this place.' Shifting her legs down from the tree, she pulled the folds of her skirt into some kind of order, and started to ease herself off the branch.

He moved to help her, his hands settling with idle possession about her waist, and as she felt his broad shoulders beneath her fingers she looked once more into his eyes and knew a profound and utter confusion.

Her feet made contact with the floor, but there was no solidity to it any more. He was supporting her, his fingers warm on the soft flare of her hips, his thumbs spanning the base of her ribcage. She might have been naked to his touch, and the sensation startled her in its intensity, making her nerves jump in riotous disorder. He made no move to let her go, his tautly muscled body so close that she could feel the beat of his heart, a steady, deep throb, so unlike the reckless tumult of her own. The soft fullness of her breasts brushed against the hard wall of his chest with breath-taking intimacy, and she felt faint, dizzy with the rush of emotions that besieged her.

He bent his head towards her, and the lazy brush of his mouth against her own set her pulses leaping with explosive and mind-shattering reaction, suffusing her body with feverish heat. The kiss was slow and gentle, undemanding, as he tasted the tender curve of her lips and coaxed them apart with the teasing flick of his tongue.

The unhurried, subtle invasion of her mouth made her gasp, her limbs becoming molten. Dimly she was aware that his fingers were stroking gently, moving over her with infinite care. He shaped the sweeping curve of her hips, and she trembled, shaken by her unbidden response to him. He made her feel shockingly alive, experience things in a way that she had never done before, and that made her afraid all at once.

His mouth tilted attractively, reflecting the warm invitation that lingered in his eyes, a gleaming enticement that lured her on towards a honeyed trap. Her breath caught sharply in her lungs. This man could seduce her so easily into taking all that he offered, and that was what made him dangerous. The warning echoed through her head. There was danger here, a deep, dark cavern, waiting to swallow her up, just as he had swallowed up all those others who had gone before her.

Shakily, Katherine tried to pull away from him, but he held on to her, and she pushed her fingers flatly against his chest, resisting.

'No. This is crazy—madness——' Rees already had a girlfriend. Alison. No wonder the other woman was so protective of her conquest. Did she know how easily he was diverted?

'Leave me alone. I want to go back now—I have to go home——'

'To David?' His lips twisted. 'You're wasting your time with him. He's no good for you, don't you know that?'

'I don't need your opinion,' she said. 'You're hard and cynical and ruthless, and I don't want anything to do with you. Just keep away from me.' She pushed at his chest and to her relief he let her go.

'You might find it more difficult to avoid me than you think,' he cautioned her, and she stared at him blankly.

'I can't see why there should be a problem,' she managed.

'No? Perhaps you had forgotten that I'm your landlord. I shall be instigating an inspection of all my holdings within the next month or so to find out just how lax your boyfriend has been while I've been away.'

'Landlord?' she repeated, her green eyes clouding. 'But you're not my——'

'Didn't you know?' Rees queried with a grim smile. 'Perhaps you've always spoken with my agent so far. That will change, I promise. From now on you will be dealing with me.'

She shook her head, a bewildered frown etched into her brow. 'All your tenants have jobs connected with the estate,' she pointed out carefully, 'but there's no condition attached to my tenancy.' She bit her lip. Or was that something else she was not fully aware of? She had left her solicitor to go through the small print; maybe there was more that she did not know about.

Rees watched her struggle with her uncertainties, then said, 'In a way, you might say that there are certain strings attached. After all, you must be aware that Digby has a contract with me to ensure that my animals are looked over on a regular basis. He made no objection when I asked that you should take on that particular responsibility...' he paused '...though I take it that he hasn't yet informed you of his decision?' His brow rose questioningly. 'I can assure you, it isn't negotiable.'

Katherine's lips parted on a little gasp, and she looked at him in dismay. His eyes were very blue, a smoky, disturbingly intense blue.

A shiver ran along her spine, and he asked softly, 'Does that bother you?'

She made no answer, her mouth and throat incredibly dry, and he shrugged, a faint smile pulling at his mouth.

'Too bad if it does,' he said. 'You won't find me so easy to put aside, Katherine. I'm here, and I'm on your case. Don't ever forget it.'

CHAPTER FIVE

KATHERINE slowly licked the last of the ice-cream from her spoon and replaced it in her dish.

'David, that meal was delicious,' she murmured. 'I was starving—we had a sudden emergency today, so I missed out on lunch.'

Watching the waitress make her way towards the table, David asked, 'Would you like cheese and biscuits to follow?'

'Oh, no—thanks.' Katherine shook her head swiftly and waved a hand in negation. 'I'm full up—I couldn't eat another morsel. But I'd love a coffee.'

He nodded, and passed on the request to the girl, along with his own order for another lager. His voice had a faint slur to it, and it occurred to Katherine that it was she who would be driving them both home later this evening. He certainly wouldn't be in a fit state to get behind the wheel.

She glanced around the comfortable old inn, noting with satisfaction the gleaming horse brasses and polished leather saddlery that adorned the walls. Their table was tucked away in a discreet corner of the room, lit by the soft golden glow of a candle-lamp.

'I like this place,' she sighed, replete. It was a favourite locally, had been, in fact, for generations. In the old days, when the inn was used as a coach stop, there were stables set around the cobbled yard outside. She said, 'I wonder if——?'

'Damn,' David muttered, 'look who's just walked in.' He glowered into his drink, and she turned her head and stared at Rees, making his way to the bar.

Her thoughts echoed David's. Why did Rees have to put in an appearance now? It had taken her all her time to get over the embarrassment of their last meeting. Simply, he had been amusing himself with her, testing out her emotions, and their stark vulnerability must have been painfully obvious to him. He had caught her off guard, and, like all too many of his adoring fans, she had fallen prey to his rakish charm. He must have found it laughable, in retrospect. After all, what comparison could she bear to the cool and beautiful Alison Bentley? It wasn't fair; she wasn't ready to face him again—it was too soon, her nerves were still far too raw.

'He may not come over,' David said, watching him, bleary-eyed, over the rim of his glass. 'He and the landlord are old friends.'

Katherine grimaced. She could only hope that David was right.

'You were telling me about your job-hunting,' she reminded him. 'What's your next move if the adverts haven't come to anything?'

He gave a harsh laugh that made heads turn in their direction, and she chewed unhappily on her lip.

'What's left to try?' he asked on a bitter note. 'I'm no nearer to finding work, and without it I can't get anywhere to live. They all want the rent in advance.'

'Don't you have any savings?'

'Not enough. It all went on the rose venture. I guess I've lost that too, because of Alton.' His mouth twisted. 'No wonder his mother walked out on him when he was a kid. He was probably a pain in the neck then, too.' He took another pull at his drink.

Katherine's green eyes widened in shock. 'She left him? Are you sure?'

''S'right. Waltzed off into the middle of the blue yonder without a backward glance.' David flung out an arm in a wide arc to emphasise his statement and his chair lurched to one side. He put both hands on the seat and it settled back on the floor with a bump. 'Boyfriend arrived on the scene, or so I heard.'

The information startled her. How could anyone do something so cruel to a young child? But perhaps there was more to it than David had suggested. Rees had always seemed so self-possessed, a loner, intent on making his own way. Could it be that there had never been any stability in his life, that he had no roots, only a restless yearning to be constantly on the move?

'Time, gentlemen, please.' The words made her jump.

Dragging her attention back to the man at her side, she said quietly, 'Have you tried calling in on the local nurseries, or rose-growers? They might be looking for someone, but haven't got around to advertising yet.'

She couldn't be sure whether he was listening to her. He came to his feet unsteadily and she followed as he walked towards the door.

'Let me drive,' she urged softly as he reached into his pocket for the keys.

'No.' He gave a sudden jerk, the force of his action making her overbalance and fall against the wooden frame. Winded a little, she surreptitiously rubbed at her shoulder where it had made contact with the sharp edge.

'I'm perfectly capable of seeing you home,' he said, an unfamiliar aggression roughening his voice.

Katherine stifled any comment. It could wait until they were in the street; she didn't want to argue with him here.

Outside the air was cool, and she breathed in deeply, wondering how she was going to persuade him to hand over the keys.

The door opened again and her nerves scattered to the four winds as, from behind her, Rees said, 'I'll give you both a lift. You can pick up your car in the morning, David.'

She glanced at him swiftly, taking in the grim set of his features, then turned back to David, who retorted, 'We can manage without you.'

'I don't think so, but if you don't want me to drive you go back inside and let Connor ring for a taxi.'

'I just got through telling you, I don't need your help.'

'If you were firmer on your feet I might believe you.'

Rees said no more, merely exerted the minimum force to manoeuvre the younger man back inside the building and handed him over to the landlord. 'See that he gets home in a cab, will you? I'm going to take the lady with me.'

Connor nodded, and Katherine said, 'You're not. I'll wait with him for the taxi.'

'I'm in no mood for arguments, Kate.'

'Isn't that just too bad?' She gave him a truculent stare, and his mouth moved grimly.

Taking her by the arm, he marched her, struggling, out on to the pavement to where his sleek-bodied car waited at the roadside. 'You're coming with me,' he repeated.

She slapped his hand away. 'Don't tell me what I'm going to do. I can decide that for myself.'

'Just as long as your decision coincides with what I have in mind, there'll be no problem.' His fingers circled her arm once more, this time in a firm, unshakeable grip that made her clamp her teeth in angry frustration.

'I just got through telling you,' she asserted tightly, 'I prefer to wait with David and go home in the taxi with him. Let me go.'

He pulled open the door of his car and, with irritating ease, thrust her inside. 'The state he's in, you won't be able to manage him,' he said. 'You've already been knocked sideways into a door-post. Forget him for the moment. Connor will see to it that the driver takes care of him.'

Seething, Katherine searched for the doorhandle as Rees climbed into his own seat. The wretched thing wouldn't budge and she glared at him fiercely.

'How do I undo this?' she gritted, but he only smiled briefly, a mere fractional movement of his lips, before he set the car into motion.

'You can't get away with this sort of thing,' she threatened. 'It's kidnap—that's an offence, didn't you know?'

He ignored her, and she sat in silence for the remainder of the journey, brewing up a dark cloud of resentment while she tried to fathom the workings of the door-lock.

At last the car coasted to a halt on his drive, and she said coldly, 'I don't live here, had you forgotten? My contract is to oversee the animals, not the ringmaster.'

His eyes narrowed at the gibe. Silkily he murmured, 'Are you suggesting that I remedy that?' Her breath hissed through her teeth and he laughed softly. 'I'll take you to the cottage in a while,' he said. 'I noticed that the intruder security light was on; that was why I stopped here. Wait a moment while I check.'

She felt some of the wind go out of her sails. After a minute or two he came back and told her, 'It's OK, nothing sinister, just a cat. Come over to the house for a coffee. I can give you some literature I picked up for Digby at the weekend.'

Swallowing down her annoyance, Katherine followed him into the house. Digby would find it odd if she refused to collect papers for him, and she didn't want to have to make explanations.

In the warm, brightly lit lounge she waited while Rees placed a tray on a low table and then she launched into the second phase of her argument.

'You shouldn't have interfered. I needed to talk to David. He was very low-spirited because he hasn't been able to find work, and his money supply is running out. The least I could do was try to cheer him up a bit.'

'You weren't succeeding too well, from the looks of things. Anyway, if he had any sense, he would be sorting out his own problems, not getting soaked in alcohol and burdening a slip of a girl with his worries.'

She rejected his reasoning. After all, David had done what he could to help her find a solution to her troubles, and from that point of view she felt that she was in his debt. 'I wouldn't expect you to understand,' she said tautly. 'You don't have a heart, only a block of stone in its place. All right, so he might have made a mistake, but couldn't you find it in you to help him get back on his feet again, give him a second chance?'

'I'm not a mother hen, Katherine,' he replied with an edge of scorn. 'I pay him to see that things run smoothly when I'm away, not grind to a halt and then swing into reverse.'

'Couldn't you give him a little more time to get himself together?'

'No, I could not.'

She sniffed. 'As I said, you have absolutely no feelings.' She regarded him broodingly. 'Perhaps it's your job that has made you that way, hardened you, so that you can't feel the slightest sympathy for people with problems, or have any understanding of the trials of lesser mortals.'

'His difficulties are of his own making.'

He spoke in a coldly cynical way, and the futility of her arguments homed in on her. She was wasting her breath, as well as her time. In fact, why was she here at all, arguing with a man who hadn't a scrap of sensitivity in his bones? Frustration welled up inside her. He wasn't open to any suggestion. In his arrogance he thought that he could ride roughshod over everyone in his path.

She glared at him, green eyes glittering. 'You don't care very much about how your decisions affect others, do you? Why is that? Do you believe that you're omnipotent? Is it your wealth that gives you the idea that you can buy and sell the people around you like so many puppets? Is that why you think you can order my career for me, decide what I'll do and what I won't do?'

A muscle flicked in his jaw. 'Are you trying to goad me, Kate?' His voice was pitched low, tinged with the harsh inflexion of anger. 'Have I missed something here? Can you be bought along with all these others whom I'm supposed to have sway over? Tell me what kind of offer I should make, my sweet Miss Innocent, who's purer than the driven snow, and never put a foot wrong in her life—what does it take to turn you from a ranting shrew into a submissive, breathless wanton who can't do enough for me?'

She hit him then, hard, a sharp, flat-handed blow that struck him square across the side of his face. His head jerked back, and slowly, with dawning horror, she registered the outline of her birth-stone ring in the angular line of his jaw. She waited in sudden stillness, white-faced, stunned by her own impetuous, ill-considered action.

Almost experimentally Rees's fingers probed the rapidly darkening area of his skin. 'That was a mistake,' he said at last through lips that were tight with barely suppressed fury. His hand closed on her wrist. 'A bad mistake.'

If she had wondered about the concealed strength in his hard, muscle-packed body, she discovered the answer now. A dryness invaded her mouth, the cold prickle of apprehension creeping icily along her spine.

His voice rasped against her ear. 'Just who do you think you are to condemn me? Haven't you enough to answer for on your own account? At your hands I've suffered constant harassment——'

She shook her head in denial, her fair hair rippling in tousled waves across her shoulders. 'I never intended——'

'Because of you,' he gritted, 'I've a record number of bruises, to which you've just added another. First my foot——'

'That was your fault; you got in the way,' she said quickly, adding with a hint of indignation, 'Besides, you broke my samples——'

'You kicked my shin and forced me into a nasty argument with a beam——'

'You ripped my blouse——'

Rees's mouth took on a suspiciously wicked slant, his teeth showing, pearl-white and very even, and Katherine's temper flared.

'The only pity is that the beam didn't do its job properly and knock you out.'

'That's exactly the kind of bloodthirsty reaction I might have expected from you,' he said tersely. 'I've just about reached the end of my patience, Kate Shaw. Since I arrived home you have done nothing but turn my life upside-down; you've invaded my privacy, and involved me in all manner of social events just at the time when I hoped to take a breather from being in the public eye——' He broke off to glower at her.

'That show was nothing to do with me,' she pointed out, outraged. 'You could have refused to take part, but instead you agreed to it, and you lapped it up, didn't you, oozing charm all over the place, having your fans drool all over you? And, as if that weren't enough, you had to drag me into it, too. It didn't concern you that I might have had to work that day, or have something already planned.'

'Complaints? From you?' His dark brows rose in a savage, jagged arch. 'How do you get to harbour such a nerve? My grounds have been swarming with people because of you; my fence was broken down as a result, my stables burned to the ground——'

'Oh, and I suppose that's my fault too, is it?' she retorted sharply, stung, storm clouds gathering like so many demons in her eyes. 'What else are you going to blame me for? I guess you think that every conceivable circumstance sent to try you was conjured up solely by me to give you a rough ride? Perhaps you think I should apologise for existing? Well, let me tell you——'

She didn't get to finish. All the breath in her body left her in a sudden gasp as he jerked her to him, his palm flat against the small of her back, and the softness of her curves were slammed against his powerful, rugged masculinity. The impact was explosive, hurling her senses into a series of crazy spirals that shot heavenward like the volcanic fizz of a firework.

His mouth fastened on hers with fierce, punishing demand, crushing the ripe fullness of her lips into shocked submissiveness. He gave her no room for manoeuvre, no chance of escape, forcing her backwards until her legs made contact with the sofa and gave way, and she fell, sprawling down on to the wide cushions. He followed her, swift and vital, his long, tough body arching over hers, pressuring her into the softly yielding couch.

She felt the rage and frustration in him, yet at the same time she read something else in the harsh, guttering flame that burned in his eyes. Something that made her nerves jump with wary anticipation. It was as though a fuse had been lit; she had roused in him a dark, angry passion, which sought to appease itself and obtain recompense in her own subjugation. Her precarious situation was borne in on her with stark, overwhelming clarity, her helpless femininity underlined in a way that she had never experienced before.

'Rees,' she said, faltering, 'maybe I was wrong——'

'That must rank as the understatement of the year.'

She tried to move and he pushed her back down on to the cushions. She swallowed hard. 'I shouldn't have hit you, I know that. Perhaps I said some things I shouldn't have...'

'That's true,' he said roughly. 'You've said enough, and now the time for talking is over.

Let's see how recklessly defiant you really are, just how deep that cool assertiveness goes. You made more than one mistake, you see, Katherine. There was a time when you let me see just a glimpse of the real woman. Let's find out where she's hidden, shall we?'

He bent towards her once more and she choked back a panicked sob. In desperation she pushed at him with all her strength and slid sideways in a last-ditch attempt to evade him. He dragged her back, pinioning her beneath him with his tautly muscled thighs, and she felt the buttons of her blouse give way in the breathless struggle that followed, her legs bared by the untidy tangling of her skirt. He looked down at her and a whimper surfaced in her throat as his smouldering gaze slid in a heated caress over her semi-nakedness.

Slowly he allowed his weight to force her submission, to inflict on her the full knowledge of his hard, masculine arousal. Unbidden desire licked at her, emotions that were unfamiliar flooded her being in a sensual tide, a hot and frantic eroticism sweeping over her, drowning her in a wave of illicit pleasure. Shame and humiliation followed swiftly on their heels, colouring her cheeks with a hectic flush.

She said hoarsely, 'Rees...' but her plea went unheeded. Deliberately he slid his hand beneath the loosened edges of her blouse, and her breathing stopped as his fingers encountered the soft, silk-covered fullness of her breast and lingered there. His thumb grazed the warm, burgeoning mound, felt the sudden tautening of her nipple, and he smiled.

'Fight me now, Kate, why don't you?' he murmured, and then his mouth covered hers once more, the indolent flick of his tongue seeking out the yielding outline of her lips, tasting the moist, honeyed interior. Her whole body trembled beneath the onslaught of his lips, beneath the hands that stroked and circled and created little whirlpools of heated pleasure. His mouth moved, gliding down over her throat, and down, down, to the creamy swell of her breasts, staying to nuzzle, and explore and brush with tantalising subtlety over the tight furled peaks.

She was beyond thought. Her body lifted, tilted into his, her fingers strayed over the hard-bunched muscles of his back and shoulders. The blood sang in her ears, pounding a staccato rhythm that was echoed in the heavy beat of her pulse.

Rees stiffened. He shifted, pulling away from her, and her soul cried out in anguish. How could he leave her now?

He swore lightly under his breath, low and succinct, and it was then that she heard it too, the ringing and knocking that had not been in her head at all, but which had been all too real. The door. Someone was banging at the door, and the cacophony of sound assaulted her like a series of blows to the head. A soft moan, a half-sob of protest formed in her throat.

Rees said, 'You had better tidy yourself up. Whoever it is sounds as though he means business.'

His brief, terse words brought reality to her like an ice-cold shower of rain, and she looked down with horrified dismay at the total disarray of her clothes. How could she have been enticed into such a mindless state that she forgot everything, ignored the warnings of her subconscious? She meant nothing to him; it had been only an exercise in domination, a means to exact his revenge for all that she had put him through.

Her fingers were trembling as she tried to pull her garments into some kind of order. The determined knocking went on, and she was aware of Rees's sharp, irritated movements as he went to investigate.

A few moments later she heard voices out in the hall. The conversation was low-pitched and she could not follow what was being said, other than a phrase or two, but the tone seemed serious, and a foreboding that was almost intuitive descended on her. An oppressive weight seemed to have lodged in her chest.

When Rees came back into the room, alone, his features were grimly shadowed, and Katherine stiffened, questioning him with dark, anxious eyes.

'That was the police,' he said. 'It appears that David got out of the taxi and went back to his car. There was an accident——'

'Is it bad?'

'They weren't sure of the extent of his injuries, but it appears that an ambulance got to him quickly after the event. He's in hospital. I'll take you there.'

Nausea made her stomach turn heavily. She swallowed hard against the bitter taste that welled in her throat, and went with Rees in silence to his car, relying on the support of his hand at her elbow when her limbs threatened to give way beneath her.

'How did it happen?' she asked hoarsely as he pulled out into the main road. 'Was anyone else involved?'

'Apparently not, thank heaven. He took a bend too fast, and too wide, and lost control. His car went into a ditch.'

She turned her stricken gaze to the window, the sombre blackness of the night reflecting her mood. It was her fault. She should have been with him; she might have prevented him from acting in such a reckless, deadly fashion.

At the hospital the harsh blaze of lights and white clinical austerity of the corridors seemed to clash incongruously with the dark, anguished churnings of her thoughts. The whole thing was a ghastly, dreadful sequel to the evening's events. It should never have happened.

A nurse, neat and efficient in a blue starched uniform, led them to an office, away from the subdued, lamp-lit ward where patients slept.

'I'm sorry, I can't let you see him,' she said. 'He's being prepared for surgery, and he's been given a pre-med injection, so it will be several hours before he's in any kind of state for visitors.'

'What's his condition?' Rees asked.

'A couple of fractures to his ribs and a broken collar-bone. There may be some whiplash injury, but we don't think that will cause any long-lasting problems.' She smiled encouragingly. 'I'm sure he'll be feeling much more comfortable in a few hours. Why don't you go home and get some rest? You can't do anything now, but you can visit again tomorrow. As soon as he's in a more responsive state I'll let him know that you have been to see him.'

Silently, after a final backward glance towards the quiet ward, Katherine walked through the main reception area and out to the car. Her head throbbed dully, a knot of tension etching a deep furrow into her brow.

Rees's fingers brushed her arm as he helped her to negotiate the darkened car park. Stiffly she moved away from him, resenting even a brief contact. Her keyed-up emotions were too raw, the wound of his cold dismissal still open and bleeding. He hadn't been affected by the intrusion of the police. His reactions had been totally cool.

'David will be all right,' he said, unlocking the car doors. 'The nurse told you not to worry.'

She slid into the passenger seat. 'How can I help but worry,' she replied, her voice muffled, 'when he's lying there broken in a hospital bed?' She searched in her pockets for a tissue, but didn't find any, and it was then that she remembered they were in her handbag, and that had been left at Rees's house.

'I left my bag at your place,' she said. The memory of that time brought the sting of tears to burn behind her eyelids. While she had been with Rees, in his arms, David had been hurt.

She sniffed, rubbing the dampness from her eyes with the back of her hand. Rees studied her briefly then passed her a clean white handkerchief, his own initials distinctive across one corner.

'Blow your nose and try to think positively,' he commanded. He started up the car's engine and it began to purr smoothly. 'OK, for a while he's going to be in some discomfort, but in the end he'll come out of it. The fractures will be mended in next to no time.' He paused. 'It could have been a lot worse, you know. He was very lucky.'

'It's easy for you to say that everything's fine.' Her tone was bitter. 'It doesn't touch you, does it? Just as long as you get your own way the rest of the world can go hang. Well, this is one time when your arrogance and your autocratic, bombastic manner have gone too far.'

'I don't think you——'

'I'm not interested in hearing what you have to say,' she cut in angrily. 'You don't care about David or what happens to him. It all passes over you because you're hard through and through, and you don't let anything or anybody interfere with your well-ordered life. People who upset your apple cart are simply thrown out on to the scrap heap like so much rubbish.'

His voice was clipped. 'Katherine,' he said, 'I'm not going to take you up on that because you're obviously distraught, you've had a bad shock and you're not thinking straight.' He drew up outside his house. 'In the morning, when you've had a chance to rest, you'll see the situation in a different light.'

Her lips compressed. 'You won't be losing any sleep over it, will you? Your conscience doesn't trouble you in the least.'

'Should it? I did what I could to keep him from doing anything stupid. In the end what happened was entirely his own fault.'

She turned on him fiercely. 'The fault was ours, yours and mine. We're both responsible. If you hadn't stopped me, there might never have been an accident. I should have talked to him. I could have made him see sense.'

'That's very doubtful. More likely you would have been in the car with him as his passenger, and now you'd be in the hospital too.'

'Then we'd both be out of your hair, wouldn't we?' Scrambling out of the car, Katherine hurried towards the house, her one intention to retrieve her bag and get away from him as soon as possible. Being near to him only compounded the awful sense of guilt that tormented her. Her nerves were leaping frantically, her emotions a tangled battlefield. She wanted to hit out, to strike away the feelings of confusion and disloyalty, of total frustration that were besieging her. For one delirious moment she had let down her guard, and he had stormed in, taken over. She could not let that happen again.

Rees joined her at the door, a frown pulling at his brows as he pushed his key into the lock.

'I think I left my bag in the lounge,' she said, and he nodded briefly, crossing the hall with his long, rangy stride.

It was where she had left it, on the beautifully carved, highly polished cabinet that housed a gleaming display of crystal. Light from a table-lamp reflected off the glass doors and threw a golden pool around the neighbouring armchair.

The chair was occupied. Long, slender, silk-clad legs unfurled slowly, and Alison Bentley asked huskily, 'Rees, where have you been? Had you forgotten our arrangement?'

Rees said, 'Which arrangement was that, Alison?'

A pout threatened to mar the perfection of rose-tinted lips. 'Shame on you, Rees Alton. But then, you always were a wicked, teasing man. I'll forgive you this once, I'm too tired to be tormented.' She hid a delicate yawn behind her palm, but Katherine did not miss the swift, assessing flick of tawny eyes as they passed over her own slim figure. A cool smile replaced the pout. 'I do hope your lady vet won't be offended if I go up to bed? It's been a long day.'

Stiffly Katherine said, 'Don't mind me, I only came to collect my bag. I'm leaving now.'

'I'll walk you home,' Rees told her.

'No, there's no need. I can manage; it's only a few steps.'

'Is that your cottage off the main drive?' Alison enquired with the lift of a flawlessly sculpted brow. 'The one with all those animal cages at the side?'

Katherine's smile was fixed. 'That's the one,' she affirmed coolly. Once the newly planted hedge had grown, no one would be able to see the refuge from the road.

Alison shuddered prettily. 'It takes all sorts, I suppose, but I should hate to have them quite so close to my doorstep. What if anything were to happen, if they——?'

'Nothing will happen,' Rees interjected firmly. 'Will it, Katherine?' His eyes took on a steely quality.

'Who would dare go against your decree?' Katherine replied, and turned towards the door. Her gaze was blind, her nerves scraped raw, the ache in her throat unbearable. It did not matter to her that Alison was staying the night. Why should that affect her, one way or the other? David had been right. Rees was a philanderer; she had known it all along. What difference did it make, now that she was confronted with his latest love? All that mattered was that she not stay to witness their tender communion.

CHAPTER SIX

THE bell rang in the ward, signalling an end to visiting time, and people slowly began to push back their chairs and gather their belongings together.

'Thanks for coming to see me, Katherine,' David said. 'I'm sorry about all the upset I must have caused.' A rueful smile pulled at his mouth. 'I behaved like an idiot.'

She looked at him, his face pale, almost as white as the sheets on the hospital bed, his eyes hugely shadowed, and she shook her head.

'You know you don't have to apologise to me. I'm just thankful that you're safe and in good hands.' Her glance strayed around the small, neat ward. 'Is there anything I can bring in for you?'

He pondered for a moment. 'A crossword book, perhaps, or something of the sort. I need to keep myself occupied—for a couple of days, at least. They're threatening to keep me in here, but I told them, the first opportunity, and I'm on my way.'

'Don't you dare to argue with those nurses,' she told him sternly. 'Stay put, and behave yourself.'

'Yes, ma'am.' His meekness was belied by the twinkle in his blue eyes, and she took her leave of him feeling a little easier with herself than she had before.

In her bedroom, a few hours later, she pulled a cool cotton nightshirt over her head, and walked over to the open window. It was another warm, cloudless night, and she breathed deeply, dragging air into her lungs. Stars glittered, unblinking, against the dark backdrop of the sky, and she stared at them, wondering at the calm, continuing pattern of the universe. If only her thoughts could be as stable, but they were chaotic, swinging from one wild extreme to the other.

David's accident had thrown her, but now, at least, that worry had been alleviated slightly. It was her altercation with Rees that was causing her the most anxiety, she acknowledged unhappily. She had been angry and upset, and had vented her feelings on him, when in reality, in all fairness, he was not to blame. Subconsciously she must have known that all along, but it was as though there was a kind of force-field in her mind that tried to block out any of the more positive emotions where he was concerned.

Rees did not like women—was that what David had said? Certainly he did not like her. She was a thorn in his side, a constant irritant, yet that had not stopped him from attempting to make love to her. For him, women filled a need, no more than that, and maybe that was what she was afraid of: that he was using her, and when he had finished with her she would be thrown to one side like any other conquest, become just another notch on his belt.

The sound of a car moving along the distant road drew her attention. Her brows drew together in a faint frown. A taxi moving along the drive towards Rees's house must mean that Alison was leaving, going back to London. How long would it be before Rees joined her there?

Katherine tore herself away from the window and climbed into bed. She would not look. She would not torment herself any longer. What he did was his concern, it did not affect her at all; she would not let it affect her.

Pulling the sheet up over her head, she buried her face in the pillow. The images of Rees and Alison that had haunted her over the last couple of days had been painfully graphic. It had to end. Her mind was in revolt. She did not care about Rees Alton's liaisons. She would not let herself care. He was a womaniser and a wanderer and altogether the most infuriating, provoking man she had ever met. It was no wonder they clashed whenever they were within a foot of each other.

Well, it wouldn't happen any more. She would avoid him the way she would a contagious disease. Just because they were neighbours it didn't have to mean that their paths had to cross. In the morning she would tell Digby she didn't want the job of tending Rees's animals. Contract or no contract, she had not been a party to it, and she would sever the connection without any more ado.

Sleep did not come easily. The heat of the night and the restless churning of her thoughts combined to leave her drained, empty of anything but a numbing weariness. It was only the quiet rustle of the animals in the grounds outside that lapped at the edges of her brain and lulled her into an exhausted slumber just before dawn.

Her awakening was rude, and violent, and came far, far too soon. Someone was shaking her mercilessly, her shoulders bruised by a firm and unrelenting grip. She coughed and spluttered and gave an incoherent mumble.

'Wake up, damn you, or I'll pour a bucket of water over you.'

'Whu—who——?'

The assault on her arms continued and the lead weights on her eyelids slowly lifted. Rees, dark and angry, stood over her. A tall and powerful Rees, his features harsh with furious temper, loomed like a dark cloud on her horizon. Hastily she closed her eyes again.

'No, you don't,' he seethed. 'Look at me, you green-eyed cat.'

Her voice was thick with sleep. 'If you shake me,' she threatened, her eyes still closed against the intrusion, 'I think I shall be sick.'

He dropped her with disgust, and she fell back against the pillows. The world spun round for a while and then, when it had settled once more, she edged open her eyes. Sunlight pouring in through the curtains made her blink. 'What's happened?' she muttered wearily. 'Not another fire?'

'No.' His answer was short and sharp.

'That's good.' Sighing, she sank back down under the bedclothes, wrapping them around her as she curled into a foetal position. 'Anything short of a hurricane,' she mumbled into the silk coverlet, 'please don't disturb me. I need to sleep.'

Without ceremony the sheets were yanked off her, and as she felt the cool air settle around her bare thighs she sat up with a jolt, drawing her legs up beneath her.

'What——?' She stared at him, wide-eyed now, her senses coming fully awake. 'What are you doing here anyway?' she demanded. 'How did you get in? Get out.' She scrambled for the covers, but he was too quick for her.

'Since you weren't responding to my knocking at the door,' he said curtly, 'I used my key.' He viewed her semi-naked form with grim detachment. 'Get up. Get dressed. You and I have a score to settle.'

He stalked out of the room, and she watched him in some confusion. What on earth was he talking about?

With unaccustomed speed, she washed, and pulled on fresh jeans and a shirt, pausing only to run a brush through her hair.

'You'd better have a good reason for breaking into my house,' she told him when she joined him in her living-room a few minutes later. 'What's happened?'

'You happened,' he gritted. 'From the moment I set eyes on you I should have known you were part of some major plan set up to cause me harassment and obstruction. Well, I'm telling you, it won't work. Nasty little tricks like last night's stunt won't get you anywhere, except perhaps an ice-cold dunking in the lake.' His mouth twisted savagely. 'They used to do that to witches, didn't they?'

'Do you have a fetish about water this morning?' she queried coldly. 'That's the second time you've tried to intimidate me with it. And what exactly is this nasty little trick I'm supposed to have pulled?'

'Don't pretend you know nothing about it,' he growled, menacing her with his steely dark eyes. 'I'll do more than intimidate you if you don't fetch up some answers pretty quick.'

'I have absolutely no idea what you're talking about,' she said tightly. 'If anyone has any right to complain about harassment, it's me. I was out on an emergency case till late last night, and I was sound asleep when you had the nerve to come in here and drag me out of my bed. Let's see how the police react to that, shall we?' She started towards the phone.

'I know all about your case,' Rees ground out. 'Of all the foul, underhanded, mean, malevolent, vindictive——'

'Have you quite finished?' Katherine exploded, glowering at him. 'You'll have to allow for the fact that it's early in the morning, and my brain isn't quite together yet, but I fail to understand why you should be hurling invective at me. Is that how you like to spend breakfast-time? I can assure you, it isn't my idea of a good start to the day. I suggest you go away and buy a parrot and practise on that. I'm sure its feelings won't be offended in the least.'

'And yours are?' His mouth hardened in contempt. 'Don't give me that. I thought I was beginning to understand you, but I don't know you at all, do I? You're supposed to be a vet, but how could you bring yourself to do something as low and deadly as you did last night?'

She frowned, bewilderment invading her head like a dense fog. She had visited David, been called out on an emergency—what could she possibly have done to provoke Rees to such a violent rage?

'I think,' she said, 'you had better tell me what it is that I'm supposed to have done.'

'As if you didn't know. What was it supposed to be, an act of revenge?' He regarded her with loathing. 'Does setting your animals loose on mine make some kind of sense to your twisted brain?'

'My animals aren't loose,' she said. 'Why are you saying such awful things to me?'

'Because your damned animals, which are supposedly not free, are running rampage over my land. They've already made steady inroads on my produce, and half my hens have been slaughtered. Lord knows what other damage they've done. Why did you do it? Was it to pay me back for David's accident, for giving him the sack?'

'You're making it up,' she replied in flat disbelief. 'If you go and look, you'll see that the cages are all locked tight. There's no way any animal could be running around.'

'I've already looked,' he said through clamped teeth. 'Two of the doors are swinging loose. Are you suggesting I need glasses?'

Katherine reached for a chair and sat down abruptly, because her limbs were suddenly without substance. 'But I locked them, I was sure I had...' She stared at him in mute appeal and he glared at her in bitter wrath.

'So now, I suppose, you're trying to wriggle out of it by saying you didn't do it deliberately? And what am I meant to infer? That you were so busy mooning over your poor, broken, hard-done-to boyfriend that you didn't quite know what you were doing when you went to the cages? Pull the other one, it plays a tune.'

She said huskily, 'I'd better take a look, see which animals are missing.'

He went with her, saying nothing as they went out to the small compound, his lips set in a hard, fierce line. Katherine could feel the leaping rage in him. It emanated from him in violent waves that were so strong, she felt she would burn up and wither if she came within touching distance of him.

Slowly she looked over the cages. He was right. She carefully moistened her lips with the tip of her tongue. 'The fox cub and the ferret have both gone,' she said in a low, hoarse voice.

He nodded, his eyes narrowed broodingly. 'And you are going to come with me to get them back.'

She armed herself with a pair of stout gloves and one of the smaller transporting cages, and they walked over to the hen hut to inspect the damage.

'There's a broken slat,' she pointed out, subdued. 'The cub must have gone in through there.'

'Another of your friend's lapses,' he said grimly, and a flicker of her old spirit revived.

'No doubt you would have him get up out of his hospital bed to put it right?'

He fixed her with a cold stare. 'Just fill the cage,' he said.

'We'll go after the ferret,' she muttered. 'Guzzler will return of his own accord when he gets hungry.'

'That'll be very soon, won't it, considering the feast he's just had?' Rees snapped, and she ignored his sarcasm.

'If you could restrain yourself and be a little more quiet, we might be able to hear if anything's moving in the undergrowth,' she said. 'Look for any place, low and dark, that would provide a shelter.'

He grunted and they searched in silence for some time, until Rees murmured softly, 'You mean like that piece of old guttering? I thought I saw something——'

He knelt down and stretched out his hand towards the opening. Katherine yelped, 'Don't put your hand in there——' But her warning came a fraction too late, and Rees gave an agonised shout, and jumped to his feet, the ferret dangling from his finger, teeth sunk into the digit like a vicious clamp.

He shook it fiercely, but it was no use; the ferret wasn't giving in. Blood ran down in a scarlet trail and splashed on to the earth. Katherine watched the colour ebb from Rees's face and said hurriedly, 'Lower your hand to the ground, let his feet touch the floor. It should make him feel secure and he might let go.'

'Are you certain you want him to feel secure?' Rees muttered, but he did as he was told. Still the teeth remained firmly, cruelly, in place, and he asked thickly, 'Any more ideas?'

She manoeuvred the cage into place and pinched the animal's foot hard between her gloved finger and thumb. The ferret turned sharply at the atrocity and forgot his hold on Rees's finger. Swiftly Katherine went into action, scooping him into the waiting cage and slamming the lid shut.

Rees exhaled slowly.

'I'm sorry,' she murmured worriedly, shifting her gaze to him. 'He must have been scared; normally he doesn't bite like that.'

'Does he know how I felt?' Rees said. 'Can I bite something?' He looked at her, and she backed away.

'Let's go over to the house,' she suggested, 'and I'll see to your finger as soon as I've dealt with this little monster.'

The wound was an unpleasant one, Katherine discovered, almost through to the bone, and she inspected it with some reservations.

'Have you had a tetanus jab?' she asked.

'Considering the amount of travelling I have to do, I thought I'd had enough jabs to cover me for everything I could possibly meet up with.' He eyed her with brooding dislike. 'If you're going to be around much longer, though, perhaps I should have a dozen or so more.'

Katherine bit down on the soft inner flesh of her lip. Reaching for the bottle of antiseptic, she said, 'This is a deep wound. You really should see a doctor about it.'

'Just pour the antiseptic and stop dithering.'

'This might sting a little.' She applied a swab and Rees sucked in his breath sharply. He muttered something, harsh and vehement, and mostly unintelligible, but the gist of it was to do with sadism and her involvement in the cause.

She swallowed. 'You must see a doctor,' she repeated. 'I'll cover it for now, to keep it clean, but you have to get it checked.'

'I heard you,' he said shortly.

'Rees...' She faltered, seeing his fierce, taut features. How could she make him believe that she had not wanted any of this to happen? She said quietly, 'I'm sorry. I wish I could make you understand. I really didn't have any idea that the animals were out. I thought I had done everything I could to make sure that they wouldn't escape. They're not ready to go back to the wild yet, Guzzler especially.'

'Guzzler? That would be the fox cub, I imagine—does his name correspond with his eating habits?' There was a hard inflexion of scorn in his voice. 'What do you do, let him have free run of the food bins?'

'Of course, not,' she retorted heatedly. 'All the animals have a carefully regulated, well-balanced diet——'

'Topped up every now and again with juicy supplements like my hens and my blood.'

Katherine regarded him warily. 'It won't happen again, I promise. I don't know how the catches came to be loose, but from now on I'll treble-check them.'

He frowned, his brows edging together in a dark line. She had the strong feeling that he wasn't about to be appeased so easily. Could he have the refuge closed down? She chewed at her lip. And what about her tenancy of the cottage? If he decided to give her notice to quit, that could throw up all sorts of problems.

'I know you don't trust me,' she said hesitantly, 'but, honestly, none of this was intentional...'

'You're right. I don't trust you.' His mouth twisted. 'After all, why should I?'

'I'd make amends—if there were any way I could... but I don't know what to do...'

'So you say.' Rees looked at her thoughtfully. 'Maybe there is something—but how am I to know how sincere you are in all this?'

'Whatever I can do——' Her glance was questioning, and he made a brief sketch of a smile.

'You'd better wait until you hear what I have in mind,' he advised brusquely. 'Knowing you, you'll change your mind faster than the blink of an eye.'

Her jaw dropped slightly. She hoped that he didn't want her to pay for a new hen hut, or for a different kind of fencing around the compound. Money was tight, and she had been certain that she had already made adequate safeguards.

'I need some help over the weekend,' he told her, and the cloud began to edge away from her mind. 'I'm taking part in a boat race at Cowes, and the man who was to have been with me has had to cry off. You could fill in for him. I seem to recall that you and Digby work a rota system, so you should be free.'

The cloud descended again. 'I don't know anything about boats,' she began, but he waved her objections to one side.

'That doesn't matter. I'll tell you exactly what you have to do.'

She ran a hand distractedly through her hair. How could she spend time alone with him in the close confines of a boat? The skin prickled on the back of her neck. 'I might be seasick,' she said in desperation. 'I don't know what kind of a sailor I am.'

'Take some pills before you come on board,' he suggested cheerfully. 'If the worst comes to the worst, I'll hold you out over the deck rail.'

She hated his grin. He was enjoying her discomfiture. He had her in a tight corner, and he knew it. All he wanted was to see her squirm.

'You owe me,' he pointed out calmly.

'I don't really have an awful lot of choice, do I?' she said.

'Not a lot.'

'Next weekend?'

'Uh-huh.'

She stared absently down at her fingers. Some of the worst eventualities were beginning to occur to her. 'Just suppose I were to come along...' She paused, lifting her gaze to him, and he nodded, waiting. She went on with some diffidence, 'If you lose the race, what happens? I mean, I don't get hanged from the yard-arm, do I?'

He looked her over, his eyes narrowing. 'I'm making no promises,' he said. 'Just be ready when I come to pick you up. Nine o'clock, Saturday morning.'

CHAPTER SEVEN

KATHERINE prepared for Saturday with mixed feelings, her mood alternating between a reckless desire to do something to escape from the situation, and one of grim resignation. When Rees arrived promptly at nine, looking fresh and clean in crisp denims and navy sweatshirt, and exuding a sharp, fizzing vitality, it was all she could do not to scowl at him.

'Are all your charges back under lock and key?' he demanded as they walked to his car.

'Safe and sound,' she told him with confidence, adding briskly, 'But if it will make you feel more comfortable I'll go and make another check.'

'And delay us? No, thanks. I'll take your word for it,' he said. 'Let's get on our way.'

The journey to Portsmouth took an hour, and their conversation was restricted to generalised topics, as though by some unspoken, mutual agreement they had decided to avoid anything likely to be in any way inflammatory. Katherine was thankful that for the most part Rees was content to listen to the light music being broadcast on the radio, tuning in just once to listen to the weather report.

'It looks like being a good day for racing,' he commented, as at last he slid the car into place on the ferry. They made their way to the upper deck and he lifted his head as though to test the air. 'Just the right amount of breeze to fill the sails and send us on our way.'

Katherine didn't share his enthusiasm. Watching the mainland disappear, she reflected that so far her only taste of sailing had been with a substantial amount of planking beneath her feet, and a healthy distance between her and the sea.

Her gaze lingered on the blue-green waters of the Solent, and tentatively she rubbed a palm over her jeans. 'Am I liable to get very wet on this venture?' she asked, and then, seeing his quick grin, wished she hadn't given voice to her apprehensions.

His dark eyes glinted. 'That depends, I suppose, on whether you rile me enough to make me throw you overboard. But don't worry, I'll see to it that you wear a life-jacket.'

Her teeth met with a snap. 'Right now,' she gritted, 'you might well think this is funny, but, if anything does go wrong, I'm telling you for sure, you won't find anything much to laugh about. If your rotten dinghy overturns and I end up in Davey Jones's locker, I'll come back and haunt you, see if I don't.'

His grin widened, and her tempestuous thoughts stayed with her as they left the ferry and crossed the River Medina on the floating bridge to West Cowes. Her jaw firmed in mutiny. He had bamboozled her into this. It wouldn't have surprised her to discover that he had set her up from the first, for some unholy reckoning that only his devious mind could contrive.

They approached the crowded harbour some minutes later, and she noted sourly that the wretched man was humming softly to himself. He wasn't bothered a jot about her feelings, he was enjoying himself at her expense. It was then, to her chagrin, that she recognised the tune he was picking out: a seafaring ditty, with throwing the man overboard featuring heavily as its theme.

Her nose lifted a notch. She wouldn't give him the satisfaction of knowing that his adolescent humour was getting to her. Instead, cupping a hand over her eyes to ward off the fiercer rays of sunlight, she pointedly turned to survey the multitude of yachts that dipped desultorily on the sparkling water. There were all kinds—from small, wide-based dinghies to the large, sleek vessels that waited regally for their owners to claim them.

'Where are you moored?' she asked, her glance skimming over the array of wind-buffeted sails.

Rees waved a hand in the general direction of the open water, and said briefly, 'A launch will take us there.'

A short time later they set off in a hired motor boat, and Katherine sat in the stern and watched the white foam tumble and crash in little breakers behind them, her thoughts engrossed. There was a timeless quality about the sea, she reflected; it held a challenging mixture of fear and excitement that tightened her stomach muscles, and energised the throb of blood in her veins. She felt the launch slowing, and heard Rees exchanging a few words with the skipper before reaching out an arm to help her to her feet.

She glanced around, and took the arm that was offered, and when she looked up and saw the craft that awaited them she caught her breath and was infinitely glad of that steadying touch.

'You didn't say—I thought——'

'I know what you thought.' There was a smile in Rees's voice as he helped her aboard, and Katherine choked back the flood of stormy words that battled for release. He had tricked her, deceived her, deliberately let her go on thinking that they would be at the mercy of the waves in a small, open boat. She had expected nothing like this. A sleek thirty-footer, shimmering like a jewel on the rippling sea.

While he stowed a couple of boxes below deck she stared around in wonder, her eyes drawn to the glossy, fresh-painted lines of the boat, and the gleaming woodwork of the cabin. Her fingers encountered the polished chrome of the deck rail, and she stood there, unmoving, drawing the sea air deeply into her lungs. Relief coursed through her in an effervescent warmth.

'Come on,' Rees said, coming up through the companionway. 'We've got work to do.'

Her attention was caught by the disappearing launch, and with the knowledge that they were alone on this vessel came a momentary wave of panic which threatened to swamp the relief. 'How do we get back?' she muttered.

'You'll be swimming the distance,' he said flatly, 'unless you get a move on and give me a hand.'

She grimaced, and realised that of course somewhere, on a boat this size, he must have an inflatable tucked away. Her spirits rose again like quicksilver, an invigorating optimism adding a restless energy to her limbs. 'I'm all yours,' she said lightly. 'What do you want me to do?'

His grey-blue gaze ran over her. 'Don't tempt me,' he advised her silkily, 'or that's an offer I might just take you up on.'

Wide-eyed, Katherine absorbed the implications of that while he turned and began to rummage in a locker. Straightening, he tossed her a life-jacket. 'Here, put this on.'

Flushed with unnatural heat, she avoided his mocking glance and did as she was told, zipping it up firmly. He was making fun of her again, and she would have to be on her guard, or she would be too easy a target. It seemed that where he was concerned her sensitivities were on overdrive.

Rees shrugged into his own jacket, and turned his attention to the sails, losing interest in his baiting games. He worked deftly, his long fingers skilful on the ropes, his strong, sinewed arms pulling the canvas into place with ease.

Katherine watched him in silence. Tall, and capable, and so obviously in command of himself, he stirred up a wealth of feelings inside her and she could understand none of them. What was happening to her?

'You can manoeuvre the sheets for me,' he called over his shoulder, 'while I take the helm.'

Her throat was strangely tight and aching. When she had first come to Fairoak to live she had been a relatively normal individual, she had thought, content with herself and the way she organised her life. But now all that had changed. There was no logic to her emotions any more, everything was confused. What was it about him that set her at odds with herself whenever they were together?

'Katherine, are you listening to me?' His voice rasped in her ear, tearing her from her abstraction.

'Sorry,' she muttered. 'Yes—uh——' She looked around her vaguely, her expression puzzled. 'Sheets, did you say? I thought they were called sails?'

A muscle flicked in his jaw. 'This,' he said carefully, indicating a length of rope, 'is the sheet. It's the line that adjusts the sail. Have you got that?'

She nodded, and he took hold of her fingers and positioned them around the rope, his own hand closing firmly over hers. Shock waves rippled along her arm like a sudden surge of electricity. She felt the crackle of it disturb the fine hairs on the surface of her warm skin.

'Wind the rope,' he told her, 'around the cleat, see, like this, to take some of the strain. You pull it, or ease it, when I say. Do you understand?' He studied her closely, his dark eyes narrowed.

Her mouth was dry, her voice husky. 'Yes,' she managed, 'I understand.' And after a moment, seemingly satisfied, he released her fingers and went over to the helm.

She cleared her throat. 'What kind of race is it?'

'Offshore handicap,' he answered shortly, his concentration fixed on the panel in front of him.

'Oh.' Her brow furrowed. 'What does that mean? Do you have to carry extra ballast, in the same way that horses are weighted?' Her eyes searched for signs of extra load, and he gave a laugh of disbelief.

'You mean, so that the last one to sink is the winner?' He shook his head, his mouth wry. 'No, it doesn't happen quite like that, thank heavens. Because the yachts are all different, there are time penalties imposed to even things out a bit. Then it's a question of which is the best crew, not which is the best boat.'

'Oh.' She chewed on her lip. 'You took a chance, then, bringing me along.'

'Don't remind me.' He looked out to sea. 'Now, are you ready? Because I think we're about to get under way.'

Katherine nodded uncertainly, and held on to the line. A breeze lifted the honeyed hair from her cheek, and allowed the sun, high in the sky, to warm her face.

Rees loosed the mooring chain and they slid out over the water, a current of air catching at the sails, and she felt a quiver of excitement ripple through her. They moved, slowly at first, the waves lapping at the sides of the boat, then, as Rees used the wind to his advantage, they gathered speed and she felt the exhilaration grow in her.

Over the next half-hour or so she began to realise that Rees knew what he was doing: he worked the helm with efficient ease, his hands strong and firm, guiding his solid craft on course.

They tacked with the wind, and Katherine worked the ropes, looking out over the water, checking the progress of the other boats. One was closing, fast, coming up alongside, and she watched the man at its helm warily. The way he was approaching them made her suddenly very nervous. He was a madman, crazy; surely he was going to ram them if he kept up that pace?

'Tighten the sheet,' Rees commanded, but he was not looking at her; he was absorbed in studying the waves, and he couldn't have seen this lunatic who seemed bent on crashing into them. The swell of the water rose and shattered, their vessel seemed to be lurching, hounded by the demon who pursued them. He looked like a maniac, she decided; his mouth was set in a hard line, his shoulders were hunched in determination. It didn't matter to him what happened to them; he was set on blasting them out of the water, even if he had to use his own boat to do it.

'The line, Kate—damn you, what the hell are you playing at?' Rees's voice cut angrily into her thoughts.

'He's out to get us,' she said, not daring to take her eyes from the other boat that was slewing in their wake, water lashing at its sides. 'You weren't looking, you didn't see——'

Rees moved her bodily out of the way and pulled at the rope. His face was grim, his dark eyes narrowed on the sails.

Katherine's jaw dropped. Panicked, she said, 'But you can't do that—who's steering this thing?'

'Forget the steering,' he advised tersely, fastening the rope in tight coils around the cleat. 'Would you rather we sank?'

'But how——?'

'The wheel's lashed,' he explained. 'Stop daydreaming, will you, and keep your mind on what you're supposed to be doing? If I give you an order, you jump to it, do you hear?'

'But he was too close, he was——'

'He was running a race,' Rees said through his teeth. 'That's what this is all about, in case you hadn't noticed. It's precisely what I was trying to do, till you managed to scupper things. As it is, he's well ahead now.' He glared at her and she bristled.

'Don't you take your temper out on me,' she fumed. 'You weren't looking at him; you weren't taking any notice at all of what he was doing. All you were interested in was watching the waves make pretty patterns. A fat lot of good that would have done.'

'Those patterns,' he said with deadly precision, 'were telling me which tack I should be following. If you had kept your wits about you, instead of gaping at all and sundry, we'd have been well away. As it is, we might just as well head for home now. We've as much chance of winning this as a blind man finding his way in a blizzard.'

'We're losing?' she said faintly.

'You got it. We're losing.'

'Oh.' She frowned. 'All the same, he——'

'There are rules on the water, Katherine. He was following them. I was following them. Everyone was doing fine.'

She gulped. 'Except for me?'

He nodded. 'Except for you. When the handicapper set the points he didn't account for you, did he? Maybe I should have a word with him when we get back.'

She swallowed again. 'Do you think that might do some good?'

He eyed her sourly. 'Not a chance, lame-brain. We're well and truly done for.'

'Oh.' She studied her toes for a moment or two. Then, shifting her shoulders back, she hooked her thumbs into the belt of her jeans, and said, 'Well, if that's how it goes, we may as well go back, as you say, and get something to eat.' She looked at him hopefully. 'I don't know about you, but I'm starving.' She hadn't been able to face food at breakfast-time, but now she was beginning to feel the pinch.

'Peasant,' he muttered, and went back to the helm.

They arrived back at the mooring, and she waited expectantly for him to launch the dinghy. When he made no move to do it, but merely stretched his long limbs and wandered over to lean on the deck rail and survey the tranquil scene, she wondered whether a reminder would be timely.

'I'm hungry,' she complained, 'and thirsty. Can't we go and find a café where they serve ice-cold drinks and snacks? Anything will do, a sandwich even.'

His glance assessed her briefly. 'Are you actually expecting me to feed you?' He went back to his contemplation of the water. 'To the fish would be more like it.'

'You're such a grouch,' she said. 'It could have been worse—we could have lost a sail, or gone overboard or something. As it was, you had the thrill of nearly winning. Besides, there's always the next time to look forward to.'

'Are you sure about that?' Rees asked with dire emphasis, running his gaze meaningfully over her slender neck. Her hand went to her throat, and his mouth twisted. 'Exactly,' he muttered with satisfaction.

Unzipping his jacket, he tossed it into a nearby locker, and Katherine watched him, crestfallen. She ran the tip of her tongue over her lips, and said wistfully, 'Why do I always finish up apologising to you? Are you planning to starve me into submission?'

He actually appeared to be considering the suggestion. 'That's certainly one idea worth thinking about,' he agreed with undue appreciation, and she made a sulky pout. 'But,' he went on calmly, 'it just so happens I could do with a bite to eat myself. If you want something, you'll have to come down to the galley and help me sort it out.'

'What did you say? You mean, you've got food on board? You knew all along—of all the rotten tricks——'

The galley was a gem, she found. Not only was there a fully operational fridge, it even had icecubes, and Rees extracted a bottle of wine that had been chilled to perfection.

They took the food up on deck and set it out on a picnic table. Katherine removed her jacket and the jumper that was becoming too warm, and laid them to one side before surveying the meal. He had thought of everything. There was roast chicken and salad, and succulent appetisers that made her mouth water. She nibbled at the delightful selection, and washed it all down with the light, sparkling wine.

The late afternoon sun streaked molten gold across the surface of the water, and Katherine stretched out her legs and breathed in the salt tang of the air, revelling in the blissful peace of the day. A solitary gull circled and called and went on its way. The gentle rocking of the boat lulled her, imbuing her with a sense of total serenity.

'I could spend hours like this,' she murmured, lazily flexing her limbs. 'Couldn't you just sail away to a tropical ocean and stay there forever?'

'Hmm. It has possibilities.' Rees's dark gaze lingered on her, and she felt the colour run along her cheekbones. Of course, he was teasing her; it was a light, flirtatious glance and it meant nothing. Why should she imagine there could ever be any more to her relationship with him? His taste ran to long-legged, beautiful women, didn't it, so why on earth should he show more than a passing interest in her? She was only on his boat because he needed a crew, after all. What would be the point of wishing for anything more?

'Have you forgiven me?' she asked, and he leaned forward and poured more wine into her glass.

'This time,' he agreed. 'I'm too idle to work up any anger.'

'Have you won before?'

'A few times. Col and I make a good team, but it was just one of those things that he wasn't able to be here today.'

Katherine tipped back her head and let the wine slip coolly down her throat. She sighed, her arm outstretched along the back of the wooden seat. 'So, if your friend had come along instead of me, you'd probably have won?'

'I dare say there are compensations,' he murmured with faint amusement, his glance travelling over her soft curves.

Her body reacted as though he had touched her, her skin prickling with heat, her breasts swelling with taut urgency. Her lashes swept down to feather her cheeks. He had only to look at her, and her senses went haywire. Why did it have to be that way? Why couldn't she have the same effect on him, to make his heart beat out a chaotic rhythm? Her mind closed against the thought. She felt oddly dizzy, a rush of heat surging through her veins to throb at her temples.

She said, 'It's hot up here, don't you think so?' She got to her feet and began to clear away the remains of their feast.

'You don't have to do that,' Rees murmured lazily, but she wasn't listening; she wanted to busy herself, to break out of the spell that seemed to be cloaking her with confusion.

She pushed back the warm gold tendrils of her hair from her neck, allowing a drift of slightly cooler air to fan her skin. Swaying slightly, she paused to recover her equilibrium before reaching down to gather up their plates. Rees touched her arm, and her fingers stilled in a kind of shock.

'Slow down,' he ordered, but the brush of his hand across her bare skin was like the lick of flame, and her pulses leapt, her nerves reacted with unaccustomed violence.

'I think—I need to get out of the sun,' she faltered, moving towards the companionway.

'Are you feeling all right?' he asked, and she realised that he had followed her down the steps to the saloon.

'I feel...fine,' she said. 'It's much cooler down here.' And Rees seemed to accept her word. He went into the galley and produced another bottle of wine.

'Do you want more?' he asked, holding out a glass.

'Mmm, please. It's delicious. I've never tasted anything quite like it; it's so light and cool and refreshing.'

She stared down at the clear liquid, her mouth curving, then she sipped slowly, feeling the tingle of the tiny bubbles in her nostrils. It was strange how parched her throat felt, or maybe it was the vintage that tempted her palate.

Rees watched her from the doorway, a faint tilt to his mouth, the glimmer of something she could not fathom in his smoke-grey eyes. Would she ever read there what she ached for? The sudden intensity of her innermost longing shocked her to the core. It was something she had hardly dared admit, even to herself. She wanted to be close to Rees, to share with him more than just a casual friendship or a mild flirtation, and the feeling was a sharp, bitter-sweet ache that tore at her heart because it could never happen.

His height and presence in the confines of the cabin was having a tumultuous effect on her. He seemed to dominate the room; he was standing only an arm's length away, yet even that seemed too far, and she found herself wanting to reach out and touch him, to draw him even closer.

Feverish heat raced through her body at the wayward drift of her thoughts, the small pulse in the hollow of her throat beginning to beat rapidly. She drank some more of her wine, draining the glass, then rested the cool crystal against her hot cheek.

He was still looking at her, in that strangely disturbing way, and she said huskily, 'I meant what I said, you know. I'm sorry if I lost you the race. I always seem to be doing something wrong, and I don't know how it happens that way. It hasn't been much of a holiday for you so far, has it?'

He did not answer, and her brows pulled together in a frown. Why was she saying these things? It would only serve to remind him of the arguments that had raged between them, and she did not need that now. The last thing she wanted was more tension between them. Her mind was floating, she wasn't thinking too clearly.

Sifting through the muddle of her thoughts, she went on softly, 'You came home to relax, to take time out from problems, but it didn't work out that way, did it?' Her tongue seemed to cling to the roof of her mouth. She was babbling. What was wrong with her? 'I feel as though I should make amends, somehow.'

He moved towards her, very slowly, and still he did not speak. What was he thinking? Why didn't he talk to her, say something? She shook her head as if that might help to clear away some of the fog. Perhaps it was the wine that was making her feel so strange, as though her blood was fizzing, shooting up sparks towards her brain. She ought to have eaten before this; it was almost as though pure alcohol was being poured into her veins.

Rees took the glass from her fingers, and she stared at him as he placed it in a well in the saloon table. When he turned to her again she leaned back against an upright beam, her spine sliding in an instinctively feline gesture against the smoothly polished wood. It was as though, just at that moment, she needed the support of that hard surface.

He followed her sinuous, indolent movements, his gaze smoke-blue and unfathomable. It seemed to Katherine that she had stopped breathing, and, afraid that he would read the glittering, mute appeal in her green eyes, she let her lashes sweep down to dust her cheeks.

He came to her, and she swayed, the slight shift of her body closing the infinitesimal space between them. His body was hard, and warm, and the faint, musky scent of his aftershave teased her nostrils. She breathed deeply, her senses gloriously alive, provocatively demanding. His arms locked around her, and her mind exploded in shattering sensation as the softness of her breasts was crushed against the firm-muscled wall of his chest.

In the silence of the cabin his sharp intake of breath was clearly audible. Katherine heard it, and wondered, and noted the sudden stillness of his long body. There was a certain heady, intoxicating delight in discovering the very real power of her femininity.

Her hands travelled upwards over his arms and she felt the tension in him, marvelled at the quick bunching of his biceps beneath her seeking fingers. Excitement spiralled in her, her lips parting in an unconsciously sensuous invitation.

'Do you have any idea what you're doing?' he muttered, his voice roughened, and she looked at him through her lashes, her head tilted to one side, so that her long golden hair spilled in unruly waves over her shoulder.

'I'm not sure that I do,' she murmured huskily. 'Am I bothering you? I never seem to do the right thing when I'm around you, do I? Am I annoying you? Shall I——?'

'Stop talking,' he growled thickly. 'You're driving me out of my head, but I don't need to tell you that—you know it already, don't you? It's all part of some fiendish plan you've concocted. Well, you're not going to succeed, my sweet, tantalising, green-eyed vixen. I'm on to your little game and there's only one way to deal with you——'

His lips claimed hers in a heated sensual demand that succeeded in banishing every coherent thought from Katherine's mind. The urgent, seeking pressure of his mouth probed and explored, his tongue darting across the full pink curve of her lip, ravaging her defences until nothing existed except for a fierce, unreasoning desire. It was a fiery compulsion that burned deep within her, a passion that only he could assuage, he of all men.

Slowly he dealt with the buttons of her thin cotton top, pushing the flimsy material to one side. She gasped as his fingers stroked the rounded swell of her warm, bare breast, his thumb caressing the taut, aching nipple, and a wave of pleasure shuddered through her body. She clutched at his shoulders, she was weak and dizzy, faint with a helpless yearning which she could neither comprehend nor control.

'Rees...' His name hovered on her lips as she yielded shakily to the exquisite brush of his fingers over her heated skin.

'What is it, Katherine? What do you want? Tell me... show me...' He moved, his powerful body shifting in unison with hers, the taut muscles of his thighs urging her towards the soft, enveloping warmth of a wide, cushioned seat, tilting her backwards into it. 'Your skin is like silk, smooth, perfect... I can't get enough of you, Katherine; I want you, need you——'

He broke off with a muffled groan, his head bending towards her breast, his tongue sliding in a thrilling caress over the creamy slope, flicking lightly over the tight-furled bud. Her senses reeled in a vortex of overwhelming excitement and wonder. How was it possible to feel such delight, such an intense, piercing desire? A soft whimper of pleasure surfaced on her lips, and she ran her fingers through the dark thickness of his hair, her body moving in restless abandon beneath the forceful weight of his.

'What is it about you that drives me to the very edge of my control?' he muttered hoarsely. 'What are you, Katherine? What is this bewitching combination of innocence and seduction? What is the real you?'

With tantalising slowness his hands shaped her, and she felt the zip of her jeans move under the guidance of his fingers. Fingers that were unsteady... She marvelled at that as he drew the restricting garment from her legs. Could it be that he was in the grip of the same breathless anticipation that held her in thrall?

The glide of his lips over the flat plane of her stomach invoked a hectic, tremulous response in her, a mind-shattering expectancy that was a mixture of fear and excitement. His palm followed the contours of hip and thigh, and slid beneath her knee, arching it upwards, his thumb smoothing over the velvet, tender skin. As though in answer to her inner yearnings his mouth brushed the sensitised place, nuzzled with a delicacy that made her pulses leap wildly.

With slow deliberation Rees trailed his fingers along the silken length of her leg, closing them around her ankle, and her eyes widened in startled reaction. His hot, glittering gaze probed their green depths, and then his head lowered once more, and she felt the slow sweep of his tongue as he tested the vulnerable warmth of her inner thigh. A shudder of fierce desire racked her body, but as his gleaming dark eyes travelled over her she tried to arch away from him, some faint shred of caution tormenting her even as she longed to succumb to the shocking sensuality of his actions.

He held her firmly, while his eyes caressed and lingered, then he shifted, his hard, tough body moving up to cloak her softly yielding curves.

'I want you, Katherine,' he muttered thickly. 'You can't deny you want it too.'

'I never felt this way before,' she whispered. 'What have you done to me? I feel so strange, so unreal, as if I'm floating, way up in the clouds, so high and far away that I'm dizzy. If I come back down to earth, I'm going to shatter into little pieces.'

'I won't let that happen,' he said huskily. 'You're safe with me, there's nothing to fear.' He kissed her, a slow and thorough kiss that sent a spiralling heat through her bones, tilting the world on its axis, spinning it out of control. The blood throbbed inside her head, her ears buzzed with the wild clamour.

Rees did not move, and Katherine looked at him, bemused, uncomprehending. He was very, very still, as though frozen in a moment in time, his face taut with some indefinable emotion. The earth was shaking and he did not move.

She said hoarsely, 'Rees...' and he drew away from her, tugging a drape from the adjacent seat.

'Put this over yourself,' he said, and Katherine bit her lip in confusion, her cheeks flushed with mortification. The harsh return to normality left her disorientated, out of sync.

'I don't understand.' Her eyes were cloudy with bewilderment.

'It's the launch,' he told her coolly. 'Didn't you hear it? I imagine it means that Alison has arrived.'

CHAPTER EIGHT

KATHERINE'S fingers closed shakily on the drape that Rees had thrown to her. She was still struggling to pull it around herself as Alison walked into the saloon, and her dazed mind was thankful that as Rees got to his feet his tall figure partially shielded her from view.

'Rees, darling,' Alison murmured softly, 'I'm so sorry that you didn't win. But it doesn't matter—we'll drown our sorrows in a bottle of bubbly anyway.' She gave him an achingly sweet smile, and came forward to brush her fingers along his arms. 'The launch is waiting to take us back as soon as you're ready. I thought we could eat at Demetri's; will that suit you?'

Rees's voice was cool, very controlled. 'No, Alison, I'm afraid it won't. You'll have to find someone else to take you to dinner.' He paused, carefully disentangling himself from her. 'Unfortunately you've chosen a rather inopportune moment to come out here.'

'But I always come to see you after your races...' Her voice trailed off as she glanced beyond him, and Katherine's heart gave a painful lurch when she saw the spasm of shock and incredulity that contorted the other woman's features.

Alison's face was bleached of colour. 'I hadn't realised that you had company,' she said tautly. 'I had no idea that this little liaison had gone quite so far.' The tawny eyes slitted like a cat's. 'I have to give you credit, Rees, you certainly managed to keep this one under wraps. Obviously you didn't want anyone to know about your amorous fling.'

Her lips were stiff as her sharp gaze flicked back to Katherine. 'You had better make the most of your time with him because it won't last, you know. You may have turned his head for a moment, but he's only slumming, and the novelty will very soon wear off. You're not his type, after all.'

Unperturbed, Rees said, 'Perhaps you'd better not keep the launch waiting, Alison. Katherine and I will make our own arrangements to get back.' He moved towards the companionway, an arm at her elbow. 'I'll help you to the boat.'

A wave of nausea threatened to swamp Katherine as she watched them go. She felt terrible. How could Rees appear so cold, so calm and unaffected? He hadn't seemed at all put out by Alison's appearance on board, and that, in itself, made her skin prickle with ice. More than that, although he had been quite content to let the woman believe that he had a relationship with Katherine, how deep had his feelings really gone, if he was able to switch off with such cool indifference?

Doubts tore at her, making her head throb with dull pain. Slowly she fumbled with her discarded clothes, shame and humiliation making her tremble as she tugged at the zip of her jeans. His reaction had been so impassive, it was almost as though Alison's arrival had come as no surprise to him—as though, in fact, he had expected it. Could he have planned the whole thing? Had he set her up in order to rid himself of a woman he no longer wanted? The cold wash of despair ran through Katherine's veins, numbing her with its freezing tide, and she shivered violently. What kind of man was he?

Did she know him at all? Had Alison been right, when she said that he would soon tire of her? Was she just a challenge to him, a booster to his male ego?

When he came back into the saloon she had finished dressing, and was sitting, straight-backed, her fingers twisting in fraught tension against the upholstered seat. His dark glance travelled over her, missing nothing.

'She's gone,' he said, and Katherine stared at him, trying to fathom what was going on in his mind.

Her throat was very tight, a heavy pressure was constricting her lungs, making it hard for her to breathe. She said hoarsely, 'You didn't seem disturbed by her appearance on the boat. Had you been expecting her?'

Rees shrugged. 'There was always the possibility. She knows where I'm moored.'

'And it doesn't bother you that she saw us together, that she was upset?'

'Why are you allowing yourself to get agitated about it?' he countered drily. 'It served a purpose, didn't it? Alison was getting much too possessive. One way or another she had to be made to realise that things had to be brought to a conclusion, and finding us together was as good a way as any of pressing that point home.'

Katherine choked back a cry of disbelief. 'How can you be so cynical? How can you talk about it as if it didn't matter? You used me to get rid of a woman you no longer had any time for, and you had no compunction about doing it, did you?' She drew in a deep, shuddery breath. 'What went wrong between you? Did she start harbouring thoughts of marriage? That wouldn't fit in with what you wanted at all, would it? The mere thought of having a woman in your life on a permanent basis fills you with dread—that's why you keep on the move, so no one can tie you down.'

'Have you finished, or is there more to this diatribe? I can appreciate that you've been through something of a trauma, but——'

'Don't you patronise me,' she bit out harshly, jerking to her feet. 'My feelings didn't even come into it, did they? Your only concern was ridding yourself of Alison in the most final way possible. I can't think why you had to go to so much trouble. After all, what woman would want to stay with you, once she discovers how you like to flit from one to the other like a demented moth?'

'You're being hysterical, Katherine. Perhaps you had more of a shock than I realised.' Rees studied her assessingly and she glared back at him with icy dislike.

'You bet it was a shock. I hadn't dreamed you could stoop so low. Why did you do it? Was it to get back at me for the animals running loose on your property, for all the things that have happened since you came home?' She did not wait for him to answer. 'It doesn't matter, anyway. Deep down I feel sorry for you, Rees. You probably can't help being the way you are. After all, it must have been a terrible blow to you when your mother walked out on you, all those years back—the wound must have festered ever since. I dare say you're afraid no woman will want to stay with you, so you've learned the habit of cutting them down before they get the chance to hurt you.'

His mouth tightened. 'Who told you that... David?' There was a dark bitterness in his eyes. 'Perhaps you're right. There may well be something to be said for not getting involved, in case you get hurt as a result.'

'But you don't care how you hurt other people, do you?' Katherine muttered. 'You use people as it suits you. You used me.'

'Did I? I'd have said you were every bit as keen as I was.' Hot colour flooded her cheeks, and he went on mercilessly, 'And since we're on the subject of how we deal with people, what about David? Haven't you conveniently forgotten him, your boyfriend, whom you defend to the last ditch? Where was he in your thoughts when you were responding so delightfully to me?'

His mocking reminder of their moments together was like a low blow, and it hit Katherine with dizzying force. 'You're a savage beast,' she whispered, and he laughed harshly.

'Aren't I? The truth hurts, doesn't it? You don't like to admit that you lost all thought of your sweetheart when you were in my arms.'

'It...' her voice faltered '...it wasn't my fault. I wasn't in control, I wasn't thinking straight, and you took advantage.'

His brow rose steeply. 'And how was it my fault that you weren't in control?'

'You plied me with wine,' she accused him. 'I didn't realise it was so strong—I hadn't eaten this morning—you must have done it deliberately.'

'Since you're so determined to place me in the role of devil incarnate I won't bother trying to deny it, though I must confess to a certain curiosity to see how the founder member of the temperance society coped with alcohol. After all the barbed comments I had to put up with there was an element of satisfaction involved.'

'You're completely and utterly callous, aren't you?' she said softly.

'You don't believe that,' he said coolly, walking towards her. 'You're only saying it because your emotions are haywire at the moment, and you're feeling confused.' He stopped directly in front of her, flattening his hand on the partition wall by her side. Leaning forward, he murmured, 'Whatever it is that you feel for David can't be so great, or you wouldn't have come to me so readily. There's no shame in that. You just have to face up to it.'

'No.' The cry was wrung from her. She could not admit to him that there was nothing between her and David. It was her only protection, the only defence she had against this man who would take her love and crush it to dust in his hand.

Love. The deep shock of that admission made her mind swirl, her stomach somersault with unnerving realisation. She loved Rees, who would never care for her in the way that she desperately needed him to care. He had always been a free spirit, and there was no way that he could ever return her love. There was only pain and deep unhappiness ahead for her if she allowed herself to succumb to his blandishments.

'Why not, Katherine?' His voice rumbled against her ear coaxingly. 'Why don't you let go, relax, and allow yourself to explore your feelings towards me with a little more sympathy? Are you afraid of what you might discover?'

Tears burned at the back of her eyelids, but she dared not let him see what, in her heart, she had just admitted. She shook her head, a wildness in the action, a desire for escape surging inside her.

'I should have done that in the beginning,' she said in a choked whisper. 'Then I'd have realised what you are, and I would never have let myself get embroiled in this situation. David may have his faults, but he's decent and caring, and I know where I stand with him.' She moved away from him, picking up her bag from the table where she had dropped it, and made towards the steps.

'We can talk this through,' Rees muttered. 'You're upset, you're not reacting with any kind of logic.'

'Not any kind that you would understand,' she agreed, 'and there's really nothing more we have to say to each other. I want to go back home now. Will you arrange it, or do I have to call on the coastguard?'

'You'd like to see me clapped in irons, like some brigand, wouldn't you?' he mused, staring at her, his dark eyes narrowed and glittering. 'I do believe you'd do the deed yourself if it were possible, or even attack me with a cutlass.' He made a grimace. 'Sorry to disappoint you, but we're much more civilised these days.'

David had been out of hospital just over a week when he came to stay with Katherine at the cottage. She helped him to carry some of his belongings through to the small spare room, worried that the exertion might strain the healing that had begun.

'I'm much more my old self now,' he told her, flicking open the catches on his suitcase and unloading some of his clothes on to the bed. 'Don't worry about me, I'll soon be fully fit, and then I'll be able to start looking for work again. It's good of you to let me stay here, Katherine. I really appreciate it, you know that, don't you? It won't be for long, I promise. I had time to do a lot of thinking while I was in hospital, and I'm going to sort myself out, once and for all.'

He reached for a hanger and began to slide a jacket on to it. 'I've made a mess of things up to now. Rees was right—I have to start thinking what I really want from life; I've dithered about too long.'

Katherine paused, the paper she was using to line one of the drawers crumpling beneath her fingers. A shadow crossed her eyes briefly. 'Rees said that? I didn't know that you had spoken to him, apart from the business of your leaving the house.'

'We talked a couple of days ago, and what he said made sense. I can see things more clearly now.' He opened the wardrobe door and slid the hanger on to the rail. 'Actually, he was pretty good about everything. There wasn't a choice about staying at the house, because the new manager was due to move in, but Rees did offer me temporary accommodation—a friend of his had gone away, leaving his flat empty for a while, and Rees was overseeing it for him. I turned him down, though. I told him I'd already found somewhere to stay——' He looked at her sheepishly. 'It was pride, I suppose, and you had said

I could come here. All the same, I thought he was pretty amenable about everything. We would have talked longer, but his girlfriend arrived.' David frowned. 'Alison, I think her name is.'

Katherine's breath snagged in her chest, pain gripping her like a vice. So she was back on the scene. Their argument had been just a temporary hiccup, and now there would be a reconciliation. It must be some kind of love-hate relationship that they had going between them, which survived his long absences and his dalliance with other women.

An aching sadness filled her. How could she go on living so close to him, knowing that he was with Alison? She felt a deep sorrow, a grief for what might have been, for what could never be.

'Are you all right?' David's query broke in on her thoughts, and she tried to assemble some kind of armour that would shield her from the outside world.

'Yes.' She swallowed. 'Yes, I'm fine.' Loneliness, emptiness engulfed her, but she had to carry on; life had not stopped, it still had to be endured.

'You must have been working too hard,' he said. 'For a moment there I thought you were going to faint. Are you sure you're OK?'

'I'm sure,' she managed. 'Why don't we leave this till later? Didn't you say you had to go out this afternoon?'

'Heavens, you're right. I'd forgotten.' He glanced at his watch. 'Look, I can leave it, if you think——'

'Nonsense,' she said. 'Off you go.'

When at last he had gone Katherine went into the kitchen and leaned over the sink, supporting herself against the unit. For a few terrible moments she thought she was going to be sick, and when a knock came at the door it took a tremendous effort to compose herself. Had David forgotten something, mislaid his key?

She dragged open the door, and stared unhappily at Rees.

'You look dreadful,' he commented, walking past her into the kitchen.

'Go away, then,' she muttered, 'and you won't have to look at me. Besides, I'm sure I shall feel much better as soon as you've gone.'

'You always did have a pleasant disposition,' he remarked with dry sarcasm, letting his glance wander around the neat room. Idly, he fingered a dried-flower arrangement, one of a collection she had made after the previous summer. 'You've made this place look good.'

He hadn't come here to admire her handiwork. Katherine sent him a dark look, resenting his commanding presence in her small cottage. 'Are you here in your capacity as landlord? Is this an inspection?' she queried stiffly. 'What are you planning to do, throw me out and install a new tenant?'

He viewed her narrowly. 'In the manner of David, you mean?'

'I didn't say that.'

'You didn't have to. I'm beginning to get a clear idea of how your mind works.' He flicked through the pages of a calendar which she had pinned to the wall. 'I understood he had a place arranged. Presumably you know where he is living now?'

'And if I do?'

'I'd appreciate the information. I need his address for some paperwork that needs to be cleared up.'

'I see.' She sat down wearily, feeling drained, the nausea returning. Of course he had come to her house with a specific purpose in mind. She had known that, hadn't she? There could be no other reason for him to visit her.

He was studying her features, his brows drawn together in a frown, and she said with a faint defiance, 'He's staying here.'

'What did you say?' It was a mini explosion. Rees had not liked that. His jaw tightened perceptibly, his mouth moving in a scowl.

She said coldly, 'I don't see that you can have any objections about that. I'm quite within my rights to have a friend stay with me; it isn't as though I'm subletting.'

His voice was frigid. 'Exactly how long is he planning on being here?'

Katherine shrugged. 'That isn't something we've discussed in detail.' Why should he be concerned anyway? Wasn't Alison flitting between his home and London, spending as much time as she could with him? A fierce stab of jealousy made her flinch.

Rees asked sharply, 'What's the matter? Are you going to be sick?'

She eyed him sourly. 'Possibly.'

'What is it, some kind of bug?'

'I told you, it's nothing. I'll be fine if you go away.'

Fine lines of anger etched themselves around his mouth. 'Are you pregnant?'

She laughed, but there was no humour. It was a harsh, choked sound, a hysteria bubbling up from the back of her throat. Your child, she thought, I'd have your child, and the tears threatened to break through their dam, and she closed her eyes while the room swirled around her.

'Is it David's?' Rees slammed the words at her, and when she didn't answer he grabbed her arm and shook her savagely. 'Is it?'

'Do you think I'm a complete idiot?' Katherine raged stormily. 'Do you think I want to give you the chance to turn me out of my home?' She pushed his hand away. 'There's no way you can do that. I'm sorry if that disappoints you, but I've read the small print of my tenancy agreement very carefully.' Her mouth firmed with decision. 'I'll even take out a bank loan and have an extra perimeter fence put in to make absolutely certain that the animals can't get out. My work is here,

I have a watertight contract for this cottage—you can't get rid of me so easily.'

His teeth bared in a snarl. 'Just remember that your work includes the animals on my estate, too, won't you? If I find that you've made alternative arrangements with Digby, you'll find yourself in trouble.'

She took a deep, shaky breath. He was determined to hound her. Did he dislike her so very much?

'You've made your point perfectly clear,' she said. 'And now perhaps you'll appreciate that this is my home, and I do have a choice as to who comes into it. I want you to leave.'

He stood very still for a moment, facing her, his eyes dark with anger, his mouth tight with silent fury. Then he turned and headed for the door, and the sound of its slam ricocheted through the silence of the small kitchen.

Katherine stared after him, a shudder racking her slender body, her mind crying out for shattered dreams, hopes and desires that had gone forever.

CHAPTER NINE

IT WAS a few days later, as Katherine was preparing for afternoon surgery, that the phone rang. Sliding her bag on to a table, she lifted the receiver, and heard David's voice, brisk and cheerful as though he was just next door, instead of a hundred or so miles away.

'I got the job, Katherine,' he said. 'I start next week.'

'Oh, that's wonderful.' She smiled, her own problems submerging a little as she listened to him relate his good news.

'You just couldn't imagine this place,' he went on excitedly. 'It's perfect, just what I've been looking for. The acreage is magnificent, and the roses they're producing are superb. I'm going to have my own section to take care of, and I've been promised as much scope as I need.'

'That's marvellous,' she told him. 'I'm really pleased for you.'

He chuckled. 'Who would have believed that an innocent meeting with a college friend could lead to this? I must ring him and thank him for suggesting that I apply for it.'

'Good idea,' she agreed. 'What's happening about accommodation? Did you manage to find anything?'

'Couldn't be better. There's a flat to rent over the main property—it's not what you might call spacious, but it's fine for what I want at the moment, all mod cons, you couldn't ask for anything more. I'll be back to organise the transfer of my things at the weekend, if that's all right with you—the owner has invited me to stay over for a few days.'

'Of course, don't worry. I'm glad everything worked out so well for you.'

She was happy for David. Going along to the surgery a few minutes later, she reflected that since his accident he had been far more mature, and there was a good chance that he would make a success of this opportunity that had landed like a gem in his lap. It looked as though things were going to get better for him from now on.

She only wished she could say the same for her own life, but at least it was a relief to know that she wouldn't have to put up a false front any longer, when really she was feeling totally miserable.

It had been hard to keep pretending that everything was well with the world, when inside she was breaking up, but now that David was no longer sharing her home that was one problem solved.

Rees had used her without compunction, and that still hurt—it had pierced her to the heart, especially since it seemed that he was now back with Alison anyway. She had been a crazy fool even to entertain the hope that he would care for her. He and Alison were well suited, weren't they? She was beautiful, from a wealthy background, used to moving in circles similar to his own.

Katherine sifted absent-mindedly through the bundle of attendance cards that the receptionist handed to her. Somehow she had to rebuild her life, put on a face to the outside world that showed none of her inner turmoil.

Coping with the assortment of patients that had collected in the waiting-room was one way of dealing with the problem. At least for a few hours her concentration would be fixed on them.

'Would you bring Barnaby through to the surgery, Mrs Walsingham?' she suggested. 'Has he come for his inoculation today?' She viewed the bright-eyed labrador puppy with rueful appreciation. There was nothing much wrong with his world. The only trauma he had to face was whether his mistress might be persuaded to dish out his next meal before time.

There were no serious conditions to treat during the course of the afternoon, only a mixture of minor ailments and booster injections to be given, but by the end of the session she was glad enough to be going home. The strain of keeping up a pleasant conversation with owners was beginning to tell on her. She felt uncommonly weary, everything was becoming an effort, and all she wanted to do was to curl up on her bed and hide away.

A shower would revive her, she decided, as she pulled off her clothes in her bathroom, and stepped into the cubicle. The tepid jet of water that streamed over her warm skin was not what she had expected, though, and by the time it changed to an icy spray she was gritting her teeth with irritation. That kind of revival she could do without.

Shivering slightly, she dressed quickly, tugging on a skirt and cream silk blouse, and sat down to blow-dry her wet hair. It was time she had something done about that shower, she told herself. This wasn't the first time she had suffered because of its vagaries.

A knock at her door intruded into her efforts to impose some order into her tumbled curls, and she frowned into the mirror. Had she forgotten to leave her notes for Digby? Surely they weren't still in her bag?

Sighing, she went to the door and pulled it open. The warm evening breeze riffled through her hair, and she stared in blank shock at Rees, tiny pin-pricks of sensation creeping along her bare arms and up to the nape of her neck. He walked past her, and she came out of her abstraction with a sudden snap, following his tall, jean-clad figure into her living-room. If he had come here to harass her, it was too much, she couldn't cope.

'What do you want?' she said tetchily. 'I don't want you here.' The aggravating man was standing in the middle of her room as if he belonged there.

'You could always try throwing me out,' he murmured, passing a considering glance over her slender form.

Her spine stiffened. 'Don't think I wouldn't try if I could be bothered.' He *had* come to annoy her; she could read it in the crooked slant to his mouth. 'Why are you here?'

His dark brow lifted. 'Was surgery particularly bad this afternoon? You seem unduly bad-tempered, if I might venture the comment without getting my head bitten off.'

'Surgery was just fine,' she said, trying to keep control of her voice. 'Everything was just fine until you came along. Except the shower, of course, which doesn't work, but I see you didn't bring any tools with you so you won't be much use in that department, will you?'

He looked at her musingly. 'You never did learn to curb that waspish tongue of yours, did you? That is...except for perhaps once or twice.' The ghost of a smile passed in fleeting reminiscence over his face, and Katherine felt her toes curl up in humiliation. An image of their intimacy rose to haunt her, as he had surely meant it to, and she sucked in her breath audibly.

She felt at once hot and disturbed. He knew he had scored a direct hit, and she said tightly, 'You're a swine, Rees Alton.'

He grinned. 'You said it, sweetheart. Don't let me stand in the way of your loosing off a little invective if it will relieve your feelings. I can see you're a little touchy today.' His voice was deep and gritty and rumbled over her nerve-endings. Her mouth firmed.

She said curtly, 'What exactly do you want?' He was here with some kind of purpose in mind, she was certain. Either he wanted to rile her, or maybe it was worse than that. Had he come up with an idea for getting rid of the refuge in order to please Alison? The thought struck her painfully. How could he be so cruel?

She wished she knew what was going through his head. If he intended to make her suffer, then he would probably succeed. She had no weapons left to fight him with; even her own body betrayed her.

'You're not welcome here,' she told him through stiffened lips. 'I thought I had made that clear—unless of course you've come to tell me that you're about to depart for pastures new.'

'You are in a rag-bag of a mood this evening, aren't you, Katherine? Whatever can be bugging you?' There was a taunting quality to his voice, and she felt her knuckles tighten. 'Is it that David is so far away? Is that what's troubling you, making you so edgy?'

'I'm surprised you showed interest enough to know that he's gone,' she retorted. 'I thought your only concern was yourself.'

His eyes narrowed. 'Now you're showing your claws, my sweet. Are you feeling deprived, since David isn't here to warm your bed?'

The mocking smile that twisted his attractive mouth enraged her. She said through her teeth,

'Oh, you think you're so clever, don't you, coming here, trying to torment me? Well, let me tell you, he has never warmed my bed; no one has ever——'

The full import of what she was saying suddenly hit her smack in the chest, and she gasped, her jaw dropping. What had she done? What had possessed her? Drat the man, he was a fiend; he had no right to aggravate her this way. She'd give anything to be able to wipe the smile from his lips, and she didn't take kindly to the devilish light that glimmered in his dark eyes either.

She threw him a hostile glance. 'You tricked me,' she fumed. 'I don't know what possessed me to say that; it has nothing whatever to do with you.'

'An intriguing admission, all the same.' There was amusement and speculation in his voice and it fuelled her anger even more.

'Perhaps we had decided to wait until we were married—that hadn't occurred to you, had it?' Her own eyes took on an emerald gleam of satisfaction. Let him pick the bones out of that.

He said mildly, 'It must have been a decidedly unsatisfactory relationship if your response to me was anything to go by.'

'That was an aberration,' she told him hoarsely, 'a mistake.'

'But an enjoyable one, wouldn't you agree?'

Hot colour flooded her face. 'I prefer not to think about it. In fact, I've had quite enough of this conversation. If your sole reason for coming here was to annoy me then you can congratulate yourself on succeeding, and take yourself off somewhere else.'

He came towards her slowly. 'You're very anxious to be rid of me, aren't you? Do I disturb you so much?'

'Your ego is bound to reach that conclusion, I suppose,' Katherine muttered, alarmed by his sudden proximity, her temperature soaring as his fingers closed on her arms and he began to draw her to him.

'I'm persuaded that it has more to do with your reaction to me. It's very revealing, you see.' His breath fanned her cheek warmly. 'There's this little pulse, here, that beats in your throat...' his finger lightly stroked the vulnerable hollow where the scalloped collar of her blouse lay open, and sent a shudder of electricity through her '... and there's the way your eyes shimmer like sea-green gems...'

'That's temper,' she said, a little shakily. 'It's what happens whenever our paths cross. Why don't you go and bother Alison if you're at a loose end, or is she too far away? If you were looking for a little diversion, I'm afraid you're out of luck; I'm not available.'

She pulled away from him, and went briskly over to the low couch, but it was not a good move. He came and joined her there.

'I'm sure your lady friend will come running if you call,' she advised him stiffly. 'Or is she the reason you're here? If you're planning strategies to make me give up the refuge, to please your—to make Alison happy, then you'd better outline them to me, and we'll both know where we stand, won't we?'

Rees regarded her thoughtfully. 'You seem to be rather absorbed by my relationship with Alison,' he murmured. 'I wonder why, if you're as indifferent to me as you pretend?'

Without warning his palm slid around her waist, pressuring her towards him, and his mouth came down on hers, warm and firm, and she was helpless to prevent the faint quivering of her lips beneath his. He had caught her off guard, unprepared for that sweetly sensual onslaught.

When, at length, he released her, she ran a trembling hand through her hair. 'You shouldn't have done that,' she said huskily. 'I don't want you to touch me.'

'Are you still thinking about David?' he probed softly. 'He won't be coming back, you know that, don't you? He has a bachelor flat above the premises.'

'Yes, he told me.'

'How do you feel about that?'

Her shoulders lifted wearily, her senses still profoundly disorientated by that kiss. 'I'm glad he's found what he wanted. I hope it works out for him.'

'But you won't be going to join him?' he persisted.

'My work is here,' she said frowning. 'But how did you know; did he phone you?'

'No, but a friend did—a friend who happens to own the business that has just set him on.'

She stared at him, wide-eyed, suspicion beginning to dawn on her. 'Are you saying—did you arrange that job?' Of course he had, he must have done—that would account for his confident, arrogant manner.

'I had something to do with it,' he agreed.

A thought crossed her mind. 'Does that mean it's just a sham, that the job won't last?'

'Not at all. Anthony wouldn't have employed him if he didn't know all the facts, and wasn't sure that David was prepared to work. I think it will turn out OK.'

Katherine absorbed that, then, in a small voice, she asked, 'But—why? You didn't have to, why should you want to do that?'

His expression was brooding, his eyes very dark. 'I think it was probably imperative that I do something, and fairly quickly, too.' Her brows knitted, and he went on, 'The man had moved in here, and that was a dangerous situation as far as I was concerned.'

'Dangerous?' she echoed. 'In what way?'

He looked uncomfortable. 'I didn't want him near you,' he muttered.

It was her turn to brood. 'Why should that matter to you?'

A low sigh passed his lips, his fingers absently tracing delicate patterns over the soft skin of her arm. The sensation made her weak, vulnerable. He said, 'I thought, when we were on the boat, that you might care for me; you were giving out signals, I didn't think I had got it wrong—it wasn't just the wine... I felt there had been something. But later I wasn't so sure...'

Katherine held her breath, her lungs tight. Why was he saying these things to her?

'I didn't want him touching you, getting close,' Rees said thickly. 'I wanted him as far away as possible, abroad if I could have managed it. When I thought that you might have been pregnant, that you and he—I wanted to kill him, I imagined having my hands around his throat. You don't know how terrible that made me feel— it was agony to think of him with you——'

Her tongue darted across the fullness of her lower lip. She dared not believe what his words implied. It must be that he had argued with Alison once more and he was searching to relieve his growing frustration in a light-hearted affair.

Hesitantly she said, 'Wasn't that... selfish... considering that you don't want me, you don't want a permanent relationship, you aren't interested in involvement? Isn't that what you said——?'

His jaw tensed. 'That was the interpretation you put on things, and I chose not to disabuse you of the idea.'

Her eyes widened in shock, and he said impatiently, 'What did you expect? You said some pretty bitter things, you know. You accused me of setting up the situation, of being a crass, worthless human being, and it caught me on the raw.'

Katherine swallowed against the dryness of her throat. 'But you did have Alison,' she pointed out hoarsely. 'She was your girlfriend. I know you argued on the boat, but she came to your house after that, so things weren't finished between you. Presumably she wanted to make up with you. What happened; did it all go wrong again?'

'Alison was never my girlfriend,' Rees insisted flatly. 'She wanted to be, that was very clear, and she'd have moved heaven and earth to have her own way, but I didn't want her—not in any fashion other than platonic. I've had some dealings with her father and his acquaintances, and that's why the relationship continued to exist, I suppose.' He grimaced. 'When she came to see me at the house I made it clear that there was nothing between us. She was...a little distraught. Perhaps that's why she admitted to setting your animals free.'

Katherine made a small, explosive sound. 'She did that?'

He nodded. 'She must have sensed that things could escalate between you and me, and she decided to create something of a rift. I'd like to believe that she wasn't successful.' His fingers travelled possessively along her arm. 'Katherine, have I been so wrong about you, about the way you might feel? I behaved stupidly on the boat, I realise that. Afterwards I felt as though I had driven you to David, when all the time you belonged with me—I couldn't rid myself of the thought that you were mine.'

He drew her to him, his smoke-blue gaze searching her face intently.

She whispered, 'I've been so confused, Rees. Since I met you things have never been the same. I never felt this way about anyone, but I couldn't handle the thought that Alison was always there, in the background, that you didn't really care for me at all.'

A groan rose from deep in his throat. His arms slid around her, tightened as though he could not bear to let her go, and he kissed her fiercely, hungrily.

'You don't have to worry about Alison, about any other woman,' he muttered, his voice rough. 'After you came into my life everything turned upside-down. You drive me crazy, you know that, don't you? You must know that. You're a witch, a siren—you've lured me on to the rocks, broken my ship so that I can't escape, and things will never be the same again.' His eyes glittered like dark sapphires, his fingers tensed, gripping her shoulders, his thumbs kneading her tender flesh.

'I'll go away,' Katherine said huskily, teasing him mercilessly. 'Will that put things right?'

She put on a show of sliding off the couch, and he made a grab for her.

'Don't you dare. You're part of me now; you've seared me, touched me with fire, you've got me so mixed up that I can't think straight when you're not around. I shan't let you escape.' The glide of his hands over her skin was like silk, the warmth of his lips on hers igniting a flame that burned throughout her body.

Somehow the buttons of her blouse slid undone, and his mouth sought out the velvet column of her throat, moved down to explore the achingly vulnerable curve of her breast. Raggedly he said, 'I love you, Katherine, I want you to be my wife. Say that you'll marry me, stay with me?'

She kissed him, a long, lingering kiss, ran her fingers through the crisp waves of his dark hair. 'I will—oh, Rees, I will,' she whispered.

His shuddery breath whispered against the smooth perfection of her skin. Beneath the layer of satin and lace his lips found the taut peak of her breast. With a low growl against the constriction he dealt with the fastening and removed the filmy wisp of material so that he could taste the hard, rosy crescent.

Her skirt followed the path of her other garments and slithered to the floor. His hands caressed the soft plane of her abdomen, shaped the rounded curve of her hip and thigh, so that she melted against him with restless abandon, her hands moving tremulously over the hard sinews of his shoulders. Pushing back his shirt, she pressed her lips to his heated skin and felt the reaction quiver through him.

Her fingers moved in delicious exploration, delighting in the texture of his male body, and he muttered thickly, 'When you do that I feel as though I'm losing control, Katherine. I want you so much, I seem to have been waiting a lifetime for you.'

She laughed softly, her hands continuing their fascinating journey of discovery, her mouth brushing his hard, muscled body, the pulse of her blood pounding a heavy, insistent beat that roared inside her head. She was dizzy, reckless with heated desire, aching for a fulfilment which she could not name.

His muffled groan rumbled against the fullness of her breast, and he caught at her roaming fingers, holding them still.

'Temptress,' he rasped. 'Don't you know just how dangerous your sweet kisses are?'

'I love you,' she said huskily, her green eyes devouring him. His clothes joined hers in an untidy heap on the floor, and he pushed her back against the plump cushions, his body arching over her, his lips taking hers in possessive, hungry demand, his tongue seeking out her honeyed secrets. His hands traced her pliant curves, trailing with infinite tenderness over all the sensitised places, and she mumbled incoherently, dazed by the new and wonderful sensations that he was arousing in her. When his fingers discovered the intimate, hidden part of her, and stroked with such devastating gentleness, the pleasure spiralled inside her until she sobbed against his hard chest, pleading for a release from this frantic, explosive need.

He moved on her, drawing her softness against his hard body, teasing her with the slow thrust of his maleness against the very core of her femininity. Her body writhed in a wild, feverish ecstasy of longing, and he kissed her again.

'I want you so much,' he whispered. 'Katherine, I need you...' With a hoarse groan he entered her, their two bodies meshing in a shattering, glorious moment of union. She felt him shudder within her, his skin burning against hers, and after a moment he began to move, slowly at first, then with increasing urgency, the coaxing, exquisite movement of his body drawing her ever closer to a tumultuous, volcanic peak of sensation. She had not known that pleasure such as this existed, but now, as the first intense spasm of delight shook her, and she recognised his own trembling release, it was as though their souls had fused together as one, a dazzling, spellbinding fusion that tipped them both over the edge into a whirlpool of joy.

They surfaced slowly, the pleasure lingering, and after a while Rees leaned on one arm and looked at Katherine's softly flushed face and smiled. 'We'll be together for always,' he murmured. 'You and me, and a lifetime of friendship and love.'

She smiled back at him, but a small shadow crossed her eyes, and he said quietly, 'What's wrong? Tell me.'

'I was thinking about the times when you'll have to be away,' she told him. 'Will I be able to go with you sometimes?'

He nodded. 'I've been thinking about making a change—there may be some travelling, but you could come along too; there should be no problem about that. I've just signed a deal for a book, and I've been commissioned to write more. It's an extension of the journalism I've always done, but there won't be such close involvement in the danger areas that there used to be. There's also an offer of a regular page with a newspaper that I'm tempted to take up.'

She breathed a sigh of relief. 'I'm glad about that, Rees. I couldn't bear to think of you risking your life; I'd be so afraid, so anxious all the time.'

'Hmm.' He eyed her consideringly. 'I'm not so sure that it won't be just as dangerous being around you. From the run-ins I've had so far, I should think I ought to take a course in self-defence, or accident prevention at the least. How am I going to survive living with you?'

She pretended to think. 'I suppose I could try to heal your wounds with kisses,' she ventured at last.

He met her gaze with glimmering anticipation. 'Is that a promise?' he asked.

'Mmm-hm.' She grinned. 'Do you think it will work?'

'We could always give it a try.' He glanced down at his chest. 'Come to think of it, there's this nasty bruise just here...'

She peered closely. 'Where? I don't see anything...'

'Here.' He pointed to his beautifully bronzed ribcage. 'I'm sure it's going to develop into something major...'

'In that case,' she murmured, 'we'd better deal with it right away.' She brushed her lips with teasing delicacy over his warm skin. 'Does that feel better?'

'That feels wonderful,' he said huskily. 'There's this other place, just here...'

'Oh, you poor thing,' she sighed tenderly, nuzzling her lips against his chest. 'You're just a mass of bruises, aren't you? I can see that this is going to take a long, long time.'

'You may well be right,' he agreed raggedly. 'Do *you* have any bruises, sweetheart? I think I may have just the medicine for them...'

Next Month's Romances

Each month you can choose from a world of variety in romance with Mills & Boon. Below are the new titles to look out for next month, why not ask either Mills & Boon Reader Service or your Newsagent to reserve you a copy of the titles you want to buy — just tick the titles you would like to order and either post to Reader Service or take it to any Newsagent and ask them to order your books.

Please save me the following titles:	Please tick	✓
THE WIDOW'S MITE	Emma Goldrick	
A MATTER OF TRUST	Penny Jordan	
A HAPPY MEETING	Betty Neels	
DESTINED TO MEET	Jessica Steele	
THE SEDUCTION STAKES	Lindsay Armstrong	
THE GREEN HEART	Jessica Marchant	
GUILTY PASSION	Jacqueline Baird	
HIDDEN IN THE PAST	Rosemary Gibson	
RUTHLESS LOVER	Sarah Holland	
AN IMPOSSIBLE KIND OF MAN	Kay Gregory	
THE WITCH'S WEDDING	Rosalie Ash	
LOVER'S CHARADE	Rachel Elliot	
SEED OF THE FIRE LILLY	Angela Devine	
ROAD TO PARADISE	Shirley Kemp	
FLIGHT OF SWALLOWS	Liza Goodman	
FATHER'S DAY	Debbie Macomber	

If you would like to order these books from Mills & Boon Reader Service please send £1.70 per title to: Mills & Boon Reader Service, P.O. Box 236, Croydon, Surrey, CR9 3RU and quote your Subscriber No:..(If applicable) and complete the name and address details below. Alternatively, these books are available from many local Newsagents including W.H.Smith, J.Menzies, Martins and other paperback stockists from 9th October 1992.

Name:..
Address:...
....Post Code:......................

To Retailer: If you would like to stock M&B books please contact your regular book/magazine wholesaler for details.

You may be mailed with offers from other reputable companies as a result of this application.
If you would rather not take advantage of these opportunities please tick box ☐

DON'T MISS EUROMANCE

1992 is a special year for European unity, and we have chosen to celebrate this by featuring one Romance a month with a special European flavour.

Every month we'll take you on an exciting journey through the 12 countries of the European Community. In each story the hero will be a native of that country—imagine what it would be like to be kissed by a smouldering Italian, or wined and dined by a passionate Frenchman!

Our first **EUROMANCE**, *'The Alpha Man'* by Kay Thorpe is set in Greece, the land of sunshine and mythology. As a special introductory offer we'll be giving away *'Hungarian Rhapsody'* by another top author, Jessica Steele, absolutely free with every purchase of *'The Alpha Man'*.

And there's more . . .

You can win a trip to Italy simply by entering our competition featured inside all Romances in September and October.

Published: September 1992   Price: £1.70

Mills & Boon

Available from Boots, Martins, John Menzies, W.H. Smith, most supermarkets and other paperback stockists. Also available from Mills & Boon Reader Service, PO Box 236, Thornton Road, Croydon, Surrey CR9 3RU.

BARBARY WHARF
BOOK 5

Charlotte Lamb
A Sweet Addiction

An exciting new saga by one of the world's bestselling writers of romance.

BARBARY WHARF 5

Now that Gib and Valerie have found each other, what is to become of Guy Faulkner, the *Sentinel* lawyer, and Sophie Watson his secretary, both rejected and abandoned by the people they loved.

Could they find solace together, or was Sophie at least determined not to fall in love on the rebound, even if Guy did seem to think it was time for him to find true love?

Find out in Book 5 of Barbary Wharf –

A SWEET ADDICTION

Available: September 1992   Price: £2.99

W●RLDWIDE

Available from Boots, Martins, John Menzies, W.H. Smith, most supermarkets and other paperback stockists.
Also available from Mills & Boon Reader Service, PO Box 236, Thornton Road, Croydon, Surrey CR9 3RU.

Mills & Boon

PRESENT
THE 50TH ROMANCE BY
JESSICA STEELE

'DESTINED TO MEET'

Popular Romance author Jessica Steele finds her inspiration by travelling extensively and researching her backgrounds. But she hates to leave her delightfully soppy Staffordshire Bull Terrier, Daisy, behind, and likes nothing better than to work in her study overlooking a beautiful Worcestershire valley, backed by a hill and a long stretch of trees – "an ideal spot for writing" she says.

You're sure to agree when you read her latest intriguing love story *'Destined to Meet'* – don't miss it!

Published: October 1992   Price: £1.70

*Available from Boots, Martins, John Menzies, W.H. Smith,
most supermarkets and other paperback stockists.
Also available from Mills & Boon Reader Service, PO Box 236,
Thornton Road, Croydon, Surrey CR9 3RU.*

WIN A TRIP TO ITALY

Three lucky readers and their partners will spend a romantic weekend in Italy next May. You'll stay in a popular hotel in the centre of Rome, perfectly situated to visit the famous sites by day and enjoy the food and wine of Italy by night. During the weekend we are holding our first International Reader Party, an exciting celebratory event where you can mingle with Mills & Boon fans from all over Europe and meet some of our top authors.

HOW TO ENTER

We'd like to know just how wonderfully romantic your partner is, and how much Mills & Boon means to you.

Firstly, answer the questions below and then fill in our tie-breaker sentence:

1. **Which is Rome's famous ancient ruin?**
   ☐ The Parthenon   ☐ The Colosseum   ☐ The Sphinx

2. **Who is the famous Italian opera singer?**
   ☐ Nana Mouskouri   ☐ Julio Iglesias   ☐ Luciano Pavarotti

3. **Which wine comes from Italy?**
   ☐ Frascati   ☐ Liebfraumilch   ☐ Bordeaux

Tie-Breaker: Well just how romantic is your man? Does he buy you chocolates, send you flowers, take you to romantic candlelit restaurants? Send us a recent snapshot of the two of you (passport size is fine), together with a caption which tells us in no more than 15 words what makes your romantic man so special you'd like to visit Rome with him as the weekend guests of Mills & Boon.

....
....
....
....

Mills & Boon

In order to find out more about how much Mills & Boon means to you, we'd like you to answer the following questions:

1. How long have you been reading Mills & Boon books?

❏ One year or less ❏ 2-5 years ❏ 6-10 years

❏ 10 years or more

2. Which series do you usually read?

❏ Mills & Boon Romances ❏ Medical Romances ❏ Best Seller

❏ Temptation ❏ Duet ❏ Masquerade

3. How often do you read them? ❏ 1 a month or less

❏ 2-4 a month ❏ 5-10 a month ❏ More than 10 a month

Please complete the details below and send your entry to: Mills & Boon Reader Service, FREEPOST, P.O. Box 236, Croydon, Surrey CR9 9EL, England.

Name: ....

Address: ....

.... Post Code: ....

Are you a Reader Service subscriber?

❏ No ❏ Yes my Subscriber No. is: ....

RULES & CONDITIONS OF ENTRY

1. Only one entry per household.
2. Applicants must be 18 years old or over.
3. Employees of Mills & Boon Ltd., its retailers, wholesalers, agencies or families thereof are not eligible to enter.
4. The competition prize is as stated. No cash alternative will be given.
5. Proof of posting will not be accepted as proof of receipt.
6. The closing date for entries is 31st December 1992.
7. The three entrants with correct answers who offer tie-breaker sentences considered to be the most appropriate and original will be judged the winners.
8. Winners will be notified by post by 31st January 1993.
9. The weekend trip to Rome and the Reader Party will take place in May 1993.
10. It is a requirement of the competition that the winners attend the Reader Party and agree to feature in any publicity exercises.
11. If you would like your snapshot returned, please enclose a SAE and we'll return it after the closing date.
12. To obtain a list of the winning entries, send a SAE to the competition address after 28th February, 1993.

You may be mailed with offers from other reputable companies as a result of this application. Please tick the box if you would prefer not to receive such offers. ❏